CAPTIVES
IN THE
SHADOWS

Steven R. Green

Captives in the Shadows

Copyright © 2017 by Steven R. Green

Digital ISBN: 978-0-9892858-4-1

Paperback ISBN: 978-0-9892858-5-8

LIC 1-4346833201

Disclaimer

"There was a time when you were not a slave, remember that. You walked alone, full of laughter; you bathed bare-bellied. You say you have lost all recollection of it, remember . . . You say there are no words to describe this time, you say it does not exist. But remember. Make an effort to remember. Or, failing that, invent."

— **Monique Wittig**, (1935-2003) **French feminist author**

"You may choose to look the other way but you can never say again that you did not know."

— **William Wilberforce** (1759-1833), British abolitionist

"Whichever figure you choose, the outcome is the same — far more women and girls are shipped into brothels annually now, in the early 21st century, than African slaves were shipped into slave plantations each year in the 18th century."

---**Rachel Lloyd**, British Anti-Trafficking advocate, former sex worker, and, in 1998, the founder of Girls Educational and Mentoring Services (GEMS).

"Congress shall make no law abridging the freedom of production and trade..."

— **Ayn Rand, Atlas Shrugged**

CONTENTS

PREFACE

T he brothel was conveniently located on a border region between competing sovereignties. It was an impressive structure from former colonial times, when alliances shifted and regimes changed rapidly. Uncertain boundaries helped every one involved to both avoid responsibility and reap substantial profit. No regime was motivated to modify the lucrative status quo.

For many of the women, the chateau was a sanctuary. Escaping across the border, they were refugees from governments and families that viewed them as chattel: brides to supply dowries, marriages to strengthen alliances, domestic servants. Their roles were defined within narrow terms; and carried stringent, even fatal, sanctions if violated: for disobeying the patriarch of the family, for going to school, for expressing whatever is defined as heresy. For other women, living on the margins of an economy, the brothel brought enough money to keep adequate shelter and food in their children's mouths. Without the work, they and their children would starve in the streets. And then there were the independents, the ones who decided that offering pleasure for a price was better than any other option, and concluded it was no worse than forced marriage. But for other women, and young girls, the building was a signal that their previous lives were over, that their families had abandoned them, that they were at the mercy of the traffickers who carted them away in boats and trucks, took away their passports, visas, and other forms of identification, hurt them, threatened them, and herded them into close quarters until they were needed. Like the slaves of earlier centuries, they were torn from their former lives to live at the whim of their owners. Human commodities. The independent women, who had made a personal life choice, had great sympathy for these slaves who were torn from their lives without their consent. But they felt powerless. If they dared to intervene, repercussions could be severe. It's business, supply and demand.

The chateau was noted for its wrap-around portico, where the workers could rest between clients and enjoy the view of mountains and savanna that surrounded their domain. Security personnel were posted discreetly at the entrance and along the hallways. Horses would frolic in the nearby corral while cats lounged in the sun or chased birds. The proprietress had a garden for spices and vegetables that the younger girls helped to cultivate.

From the main entrance, a client passed through a foyer where boots, hats, umbrellas, and overcoats where left with the wardrobe assistant, a perky young girl with a welcoming smile. Through another set of doors, the guest entered the ballroom area. At the far corner, a large piano stood beside a raised stage. The music varied to enhance the mood of the hour: soft morning melodies, romantic daytime measures, engaging jazz or somber symphonic pieces. Having converted as many rooms as possible, the proprietress was able to boast of fifteen luxurious bedchambers, on the second and third floors. For the wealthier client, there were rooms with bathrooms; otherwise, the hallway facilities were sufficient, a journey which often led to memorable encounters. The proprietress had her own room in the rear, with a patio from which she could follow the winding road before it circled onto her property. Her boyfriend, the head of security, was a burly man with a serious air that she managed to soften in the evening. When he entered her room, she was scanning the road. He walked to her and stroked her shoulders. She let out a subtle hum. He knew she was troubled by some of her clients.

"They always want the young girls," she murmured with tense jaws. "And young girls get older."

"Free market," replied her consort. "Supply and demand." He nibbled her neck. "I try to not notice."

****

The truck rushed around the winding roadway, the driver having little concern for his fragile cargo. The whores on the porch watched casually as the truck halted at the entrance gate and a side door was pulled open by one of the attendants who had traveled with the group. The frightened girls were huddled against each other, having rapidly become close friends in their dire circumstances. A woman emerged from the passenger side of the truck's cabin and faced the girls. "Out now!" she ordered. "Hurry!" When they delayed, one of the male attendants, holding a cane, repeated her order with deeper threatening tones. They came out like a reluctant river, some were whimpering, others were sobbing heavily, some silently glared at their slavers with a simmering hate.

When the new shipment was dropped at the chateau door, Sabrina was on the porch. She watched as the human cargo was taken into the foyer: Girls, mostly, but some no more than seven or eight years old. Sabrina rose from her wicker lounge chair and went to her room. As an independent, she had some privileges. The madam had designated her as a "bottom", an experienced professional who would train the young ones, explain the situation to them, teach them about makeup and clothing, and prepare them for the men. She was assigned to be a surrogate parent, a role model, who would then send them to the slaughter. Trusting the bottom, these girls would again be traumatized by betrayal. "But not this time," thought Sabrina. Gizem was in the ballroom witnessing the drop-off until Sabrina took her hand. The girl had been staying with Sabrina for several months and had learned to accept her mentor's direction without question. Sabrina went to the corner table by her bed and removed her cell phone from a drawer.

When she finished her call, Sabrina proceeded to the ballroom. The madam welcomed the girls to their new home while two security guards, holding rattan canes, stood alongside her. She ordered the girls to strip from their "old rags". Any girl who was reluctant to disrobe got snaps of the rattan on the hardwood floor as a warning. Sabrina knew madam would be averse to scarring the merchandise; but the threat was effective. It was essential that the transfer be efficient and rapid. Naked, quivering, and weeping, each girl was handed a towel so she could take a shower.

Sabrina recalled Gizem's first day. The girl did not cry or whimper. Staring at her complexion and hair, Sabrina imagined she was gazing at a reflection of her own younger self. Despite her nakedness, she had stood firm and stout, with her dark silken hair reaching to her knees. She glared into the eyes of the security guards who held the rattan sticks next to her.

Sabrina remembered that, in one hand, Gizem held a doll. It was a decrepit thing, which the girl probably found in a trash heap. The girl took the towel and turned to follow the others. The guard reached out to grab the doll. "No!" shouted the girl, not in fear but with determination. For such disobedience, the girl deserved a caning of her arm that defiantly held the doll. The guard raised his stick.

"Wait!" Sabrina held up her hand and approached the guard. "No need for that. She doesn't understand. I'll take care of her. It's my job."

The madam turned to Sabrina in surprise. "She may be trouble. She's strange." In other words, the girl stood her ground, did not tremble or plead, and glared defiantly at her captors.

Sabrina applied the best sneer she could manage. "Some men will enjoy that challenge," she replied. The madam smirked and gave her nod of approval.

Sabrina offered her hand to the strange little girl. "Come with me." Seeing Sabrina as the best of bad options, the girl complied.

Sabrina had taken the girl into her room and sat her next to a water pitcher and basin. She poured warm water into the basin and submerged a washcloth. After wringing out the cloth, she wiped the girl's face and hands. "Poor child," she whispered. "Where are you from?" After a substantial pause, the girl took a chance on trusting her. She said her name was Gizem. She was from over the national border. She had many siblings and her family was too poor to feed them. Her father sold her to a man who promised gentle care. The girl didn't think she was going away for good. She expected to be a maidservant for a while to a wealthy matron.

Sabrina shook her head and reached for a hairbrush. She had to pull a lot of snags and tangles but the girl didn't seem to mind. The girl looked at Sabrina's arms and touched them. "You are from my people," noted the girl. "You're one of us?"

****

The military burst into the brothel before the guards had time to react. Since they knew about the madam's observation balcony, they came in from the other side. Again the girls screamed and tried to hide. But this time, women in United Nations uniforms also entered. They identified themselves with official badges. Their helmets were light blue with the white symbol of the earth surrounded by two olive branches. The madam and her staff were rounded up. They weren't frightened; they knew the arrest would be brief. In fact, she argued with several of the soldiers over their breach of contract. The workingwomen were also arrested but taken into different vans. In one of the vans, Sabrina spoke to a female officer and requested that Gizem, and her doll, stay with her. Sabrina knew that the rescuers often became persecutors; but this woman was trustworthy. The officer smiled and nodded. "Yes, of course," she whispered.

There were international agreements. When it came to the trafficking of minors, some actual enforcement had been achieved. After a round of interrogation, most of the women were returned to the chateau.

For decades, the issue of human trafficking had been debated at global conferences. Even the definition was in dispute. Is it trafficking when ambitious laborers are willingly transported across borders, for a substantial fee, to work as illegal aliens? Is it trafficking if the person gives consent? Is the consent obtained through coercion? If a woman willingly engages in prostitution, with full consent, should she be considered a victim? How many people actually make life choices free from economic pressures?

The officer entered Sabrina's room and closed the door. She sat next to Sabrina and handed her a set of papers. "You know they'll be out of jail soon." Sabrina nodded. "You can't stay here. It won't be safe. And that gang of traffickers has strong connections."

"So. Time for me to move on again."

The officer glanced at Gizem, who was cowering in a corner and fidgeting with her hair. "Are you taking the girl?"

"This one, yes. She belongs with me. She can't go back home. Honor killing."

The officer grunted. "Such an evil term. Honor killing. Murdering the victim because the patriarch is embarrassed." But the woman understood and didn't argue with her. "The papers will work." She embraced Sabrina. "We will always be grateful. You're a saint."

Sabrina laughed at the irony in that remark. "I'm not the only one. Remember. There are others," she declared. "The New Selijuk Party wants true freedom: Freedom of thought, freedom to choose our religious beliefs or to choose none, freedom to state our own opinions, freedom for women and men to live full lives. Be good to us."

The officer nodded and smiled. "To the Oksoko!" Sabrina repeated the cheer. Emboldened by their display, Gizem approached the woman with a quizzical expression. "Your accent, it confuses me," said the girl. "Where are you from?"

"I'm from Sweden," answered the woman. "I met Sabrina about a year ago. You have a brave protector."

"Do you know about Ataturk?" asked the girl.

The officer was impressed by the child's grasp of history. "Let's just say that I know World War One did not end completely in 1918. Your Ataturk established a secular Turkish Republic."

Gizem processed her answer and added a supplement. "The Selijuk Empire was much larger. Turkey, Iran, Iraq, and the Levant." The officer listened to the precocious child with interest. Sabrina smiled with pride at her protégé. "And the Kurds have earned a seat at the table. The old useless conflicts must stop."

"So," noted the officer, "Tolerance for all."

Both Sabrina and Gizem grumbled their discontent. The officer was confused. Sabrina clarified. "To speak of 'tolerance' is to be condescending. It is the term used by a dominant master trying to be kind to inferiors. Spinoza taught us that. Drop tolerance. We want Universal Freedom!"

"Spinoza," noted the officer. "You speak of a Jew from the Middle Ages. Now I am even more impressed."

"His values are for all ages," replied Sabrina. "He rejected the concept of a 'Chosen People' and advocated for all people."

Gizem snickered. "So his own people despised him!"

"Indeed," said the officer. "Whenever a leader transcends his own tribe, he becomes a threat to authority. Joan of Arc saved her country and then was turned over to the enemy. Jesus spoke of universal love and became a threat to the Romans. John F. Kennedy and Nikita Khrushchev worked to end the Cold War and…"

"Yes," Sabrina concurred. "But this time, it can be different. There is a terrible void in the region. Tribal rivalries, sharia law, nationalistic frenzy, atavistic superstitions, archaic resentments…"

"And you think your New Selijuk Party can tie all those strands together? That is a very large dream."

"You have to dream large," answered Gizem. She had been taught well.

"But for now," added Sabrina, "We save the children and the women. That mission can unite us all together. We create a global community of liberated people with open minds. From that new community, any dream is possible."

1

Desire

S abrina keeps reassuring me. "You're not a pimp, Barry. You're my driver and my protector. And I love you for that. Really." When I think about it logically, I know she's right. I never take her money. She offered me a regular salary and I accepted that. I never forced her to do anything; she's an independent, completely freelance. Our relationship comes with a set of expectations that transcends normal man-woman intimacies. I have to accept that she sleeps with other men (and also gets very personal with women now and then). There's no place for jealousy or possessiveness in our covenant.

And yet, there are some aspects that render me a "good" pimp. I worry about her. I monitor her contacts. I'm only a phone call away if she needs help. My presence sends a clear message to her johns: play nice. Brin explains that that makes me her guardian, nothing more or less.

So, at a discreet distance, I sit in my parked car and await her call. I play little mind games with myself, making predictions about her customers. That guy is gonna pay for extended time. That one is gonna be brief. I bet he's divorced and getting back into singlehood. Oh, for sure, this guy is a virgin! But people can be unpredictable. I score about 80%. For one thing, Sabrina is very selective. She filters her customers carefully. She also has a regular clientele who know me and send me a quick nod.

So how does a middle-aged insurance rep end up moonlighting with a job like this? Maybe approaching 50 got to me. Maybe Adrienne's mushrooming spirituality, at the cost of anything erotic, put me over the brink. When the software sector crashed in 2000, and I was suddenly an aged-out techie, my solid foundation was fractured. But most of all, it was the lure of the Late-Night City.

Every city is really three cities. The Morning City is a red sunrise, a fresh new beginning. It's the time to breathe in fresh air and appreciate bird songs. It's when the joggers rule; when you can forestall the commute into madness and focus your mind in meditation or a good workout at the gym. If you think about The Triple Goddess, it's the time of the Maiden, the Virgin, the wide-eyed innocent child leaping into life. The Morning City sings with optimism and potential.

Then you have the Mid-Day City, the peak time for productive, goal-driven activity. It's the Mother goddess, tending to responsible tasks. Commuting into traffic jams, getting to work or school on time. Shopping, planning, rushing, catching a lunch break, making a conference, keeping appointments, hitting deadlines, making investments, playing the odds, watching news reports, getting to the bank. Extracurricular events and homework. Impatient scrambles, robotic, mindless routines. Noise!

We find our salvation in the Late-Night City. It's Hecate, Darkness and vampire nightmares. The average bourgeois citizen hits the bed, usually too tired to do anything but sleep. Night creatures, crickets and other chirpers provide the soundtrack. Voices carry further so conversations are more subdued. It's the time of the stray cat. The air, now corrupted by the dramas of the day, carries a sense of secrets, conspiracies, illicit exchanges, and discreet deals. The persona of daytime surrenders to the shadow of something more primal, more authentic, more animal. Civilized demeanor melts into a communal paranoia, filled with side-glances and hyper-attentive nuance. Existential, man! The raw truth!

I need the Late-Night City to balance out the banal tedium of my bourgeois existence. The two poles need each other. I love Adrienne. I love my three kids. I tolerate my job. I pay my share of the household bills. Then I look in the mirror and wonder, "Who the hell are you?" I feel depleted, defeated, de-fanged. But as soon as I enter the alternate reality of the Dark, I'm re-ignited. Energy flows, I'm alert, I'm responsive.

Brin and I are a team. Our mission is to provide some measure of release and pleasure to a population of customers beaten down by the factory we call modern life. For a reasonable price, they get to share a fantasy with her for a while; to enjoy a playful conversation, a confident seduction with a clear conclusion, a sharing of bodies for the purpose of sweet oblivion. She keeps a very limited workload. Most of her johns seem content when they depart. Occasionally, one will be filled with remorse and shame after their encounter. Like I said before, I can predict outcomes most of the time.

I've watched as Sabrina comforts these guilt-ridden souls. She tells them they're real men with real needs. She says they made a healthy decision to attend to the demands of their bodies. She affirms the beautiful miracle of sexuality. By the time they leave, they've been nurtured to a level of certainty bordering on ecstasy. Her regulars are nice enough, and wealthy enough, to keep us both happy.

Every now and then, she tells me her next customer is "political". I get the message. I then have to keep my presence very low-key. It's better if I don't know his (or her) identity; for my own safety as well as his. She reminds me to keep my cell phone fully charged. Well-connected political power and wealth may come with extra variables.

****

It seems like I had this arrangement my entire life. But it was really only three years. I was celebrating my 45th birthday, and several old friends attended the party, when questions were sparked. The music of our college days was played, and I realized we had become fossils. Coming of age in the '70s and '80s, I grew up in the ruins of the Hippie cultural revolution, when disco and punk were competing for my consciousness. At that birthday celebration, as I drank with old friends and listened to the background of classic rock, the Bee Gees, Donna Summer, David Bowie, and the Ramones, I felt like I was reading my own epitaph. We had to scrounge around for new jobs after the tech crash, and then sweep up the dust from the trauma of 9/11 and somehow move on. In the blink of an eye, we went from asking about "the peace dividend" to expanding military efforts in strange lands. I didn't look back on my history with a pleasant sense of nostalgia; it was more of a deep spiral of uncertainty and meaninglessness.

Maybe it was 9/11 that drove Adrienne into more and more spirituality. While I plunged into an existential skepticism, she sought a universal connection. We were never religious, but we did get into meditation. It reduces the noise in your head, calms you down, and helps you to see clearly, to pierce through all the ancillary distractions and confusions of daily life. It helped a lot when I was a programmer. Like Occam's razor, it enables you to cut to the chase and find efficient solutions to complex queries.

Getting silly from the booze and a few tokes of weed, we began to joke about relationships, marriage, parenting, and related frustrations. When my jokes about sexual conflicts weren't very funny, one of my buddies, in the mode of sarcastic drunk, made a remark that held more wisdom than expected. "If you guys are into meditation, why don't you go Tantric?" I had heard about tantric sex in casual asides but never studied it.

I explored Internet sites and visited yoga centers in a search of more information. Finally, at a weekend retreat in the Berkshires, at their bookstore, I found a sourcebook on Tantra. It apparently is the foundation from which yoga, or sama, emerged. It has a lot to do with the goddess Shakti and her consort Shiva. The energy of their union is profound. The manual was very detailed and obsessive. Everything had symbolic value, be it a finger position or a manner of breathing. I learned about mantras, malas, mudras and mandalas. The serpentine kundalini path through chakras, with their levels of consciousness, intrigued me.

Then I discovered a chapter that troubled me. Desire, or Kama, is what drives the kundalini energy toward higher states. The tantric perspective on desire is just as ambivalent as other religions. Tantra accepts desire as the primary force in the universe. It also recognizes that suppression of desire leads to imbalance and disease. However, desire leads to attachment and yearning for any desired object. In Buddhism, they call this craving "duka" and describe it as the source of human suffering. Moving through the chakras to higher levels, you learn that desire is not a personal thing, but a universal force, that actually liberates us from material attachments. So, by the time you reach the seventh chakra, you are in a divine realm.

Here's where I struggled. Buddha saw craving and attachment as the causes of all human suffering. So we should detach from all things that are, by nature, impermanent. Judeo-Christian prophets tend to be repulsed by the sins of desire. And yet, tantra states that Shiva without his Shakti is a dead thing! In their union is the energy of the universe!

Could this be the problem I face with Adrienne? Could it be that, as she rises through the chakras in her search for spirit, her kama, or libido, diminishes? Are all the symbols of "enlightenment" -- the deific images, the prayer beads, the chants, the meditations -- some grand rationale for loss of desire? Tantra celebrates the union of male and female energies; yet it also guides you to higher chakras that take you beyond the "distraction" of desire.

My mind yells out in protest. If you want to follow that path beyond desire, go right ahead. But a sense of the sacred can also be reached in union with a passionate partner. Lovemaking, when done well, can melt boundaries, suspend ego, and carry you into another realm of being. In my time with Sabrina, I learned about "red" Tantra that takes the alternate path. It was not a path Adrienne would follow.

****

As I drive Sabrina from her "date" back to her apartment, I think about how my city changed. Times Square used to be the "escape valve" for the city. Now it's a distorted Disneyland or

Sesame Place. In the seventies, the lower West Side, the leather bars, and the piers were dangerous detours that nourished the denizens at the margins. Now, that subculture is gone or dispersed elsewhere, defeated by rising rents and the frantic AIDS crisis. The Highline is now a squeaky-clean tourist attraction that rises over Washington Street. The old ramrod bars are gone, replaced by yuppie boutiques and expensive restaurants for the wealthy traveler.

Now it's all so "nice". Every neighborhood is besieged by jackhammers and cranes. It's all being transformed into a stage set, background for the super-rich. The class war is over. The oligarchy won. While the actual workers struggle to avoid evictions and late notices, the nobility swim in unimaginable realms of luxury.

I share my thoughts with Sabrina as I drive. After three years, I'm still intrigued by her crusade and her mysterious "network" of idealists. Even though our pattern is now routine, questions still arise. "Brin, why did you pick me? That night at the bar? What made me stand out for you?"

Sabrina always laughs at my "puritanical Western hang-ups". But she respects my struggle and strives to soothe me. After all, reassuring older guys is part of her modus operandi. "That night at the bar, I saw it in your eyes. You were suffering the same thing as I. Despite family, friends, work, and colleagues, you carried it around like a scarlet letter. Loneliness. I know loneliness." She starts to cry. Despite the traumas of her life, her covert intrigue, and her chosen profession, she remains a beautifully sensitive woman.

I pull the car to a stop and we embrace. "With you, I can take off the mask. We can stop performing and just BE with each other. We can accept the Animal but also get fed with compassion, understanding. No judging, no condemning, no devaluing. Just two people stepping out of the box to share being alive in this crazy unpredictable world."

People cling to their cell phones and their online postings. They binge on alcohol and drugs and shopping; anything to avoid the painful reality of loneliness. People desperately search for human closeness but also avoid it. The "working woman" fills a void in any culture that sets tight parameters around "acceptable" or "appropriate" behavior. The basic human instinct for orgasmic release is defined as sin. So "good" people resort to lies. Mostly, they lie to themselves with all sorts of mental maneuvers: denial, projection, deflection, or rationalization. But we now have the technology to break those walls. For every Internet site that shuts down its "Adult Personal" section, another site slips into the ether.

The same technology that keeps us in separate bubbles can also bring us together. The three cities, eh? During the "normal" daytime hours, we avoid eye contact with strangers by clicking into our accounts on Facebook and Twitter. But in the Night City, the technology serves the opposite function: it invites the stranger, the alien, into your world.

This beautiful dark mystery that is Sabrina was my ticket to that other realm, a parallel universe.

2

The Family Meeting

There's a time, in every family, when you know things will never be the same. It was unusual for us all to be seated around the dining room table, but this was our last dinner together before Amanda headed off for college. Adrienne sat at the head of the table, closest to the kitchen, eager to launch the ritual she had suggested. On this moment of significant change for our family, each member would share thoughts. To get the ball rolling, Adrienne agreed to go first.

"My dear Amanda," she began. "I was twenty-seven years old when you came into the world. Your Dad was a young computer programmer and I was a nurse, so you'd think we knew what we were doing. No way!" The family chortled on cue. "You were so fragile, we thought you'd break! But somehow, all three of us survived. And now, my first-born child is leaving the nest. It seems like only yesterday. Life happens so fast." Adrienne paused and seemed to be near tears. From the chair next to her, I took her hand. But Adrienne shook my hand away in a rather brisk manner. "I'm OK," she insisted. She concluded her comments. "Looking at you now --- a mature, responsible, intelligent young woman --- I know we did something right." Mandy blushed, lowered her eyes, and thanked her mother.

Candice took the next turn. "Hey, Mandy. I know I was the annoying younger sister sometimes. I know because you said so." Giggles. Glenn jumped in with, "Yeah! I heard them!" I put my finger to my lips and Glenn sat back quietly. Candi continued. "Anyway, there were so many times you brushed my hair, and you helped me with math homework. You showed me a lot about makeup, at least until Mom became a beautician."

"Don't you mean a cosmonaut?" asked Glenn sarcastically.

"No," Candice countered. "Cosmologist!" She and her brother giggled. Amanda glared at Candice, who got the message. "Sorry, Mom. When Mom became a cosmetologist," she said each syllable carefully, "I had double the help. You helped me get on the cheerleader squad! But you also recognized my writing ability and encouraged me to work in the school newspaper. But science, wow! That was your specialty, big sister! Chemistry! Quantum Physics! Omigod! You're awesome! And sometimes, when my social life really sucked, you were there. I love you, Mandy." Amanda walked over and gave her sister a hug.

Then it was Glenn's turn. "When Mom worked as a nurse, and had night hours, you took care of me. Hoboy!" All the participants snickered at that lament. "A time limit on video games. I had to help with washing the dishes. You made me get all my homework done. You were tough! But, you know what? You were right. I did well in school. I should help out. And, yeah, thanks for the help with math." Glenn and Amanda shared a high-five.

All eyes turned to me. A torrent of ideas raced in my thoughts. I had to focus, be coherent, and launch my daughter with positive energy. "I'm so proud of you, baby. But that sounds so typical, so rehearsed. You deserve much more than that." Memories flooded from all sides. "When your Mom and I were stressed out, when we got into arguments, you intervened. I never wanted to put that responsibility on you, but you did it out of love. When we both went through our career changes, you were always there to pick up the slack. So, I'm glad you're escaping from us." The mirth was infused with a few drops of anxiety. "I really mean that. You need to have your time to live your own life." The eye contact between

Amanda and myself was intense. "You took care of us so well that we sometimes missed your cries for help." Amanda shook her head and spoke to reassure me. But I wanted to let her know how much I appreciated her. "But there were times, very close times, when we heard you. I'm glad we did. And what a resilient, intelligent, assertive woman you've become! Such a capacity to listen and learn, to love and be loved, to follow your dreams with determination. Yes, I am very proud of you."

"Oh, Dad!" Amanda rose from her chair with tears in her eyes and rushed into my arms.

I held her close to me and said, "But you're still our baby. If you need anything, you let us know." She agreed to do so.

The meeting soon disintegrated into cell phones, TV, and checkbooks. As I checked my current bank balances, Adrienne approached with a stern expression. "What?"

"Did you really have to bring up all the garbage?"

"That's not fair. I was letting her know how much I appreciate…"

"The arguments. The job changes and the downsizing. Really? You had to remind her what lousy parents we were?"

"I didn't say that."

"So she has to escape from us, eh?"

With no further discourse, Adrienne scrambled to the TV room to enjoy the drama of a TV family. And, of course, Amanda witnessed the encounter. She hurried to me and started to speak but I stopped her.

"Listen, baby. Like I said, don't jump into our muddle any more. We'll survive. I'll smooth her feathers. You have to go upstairs and finish packing." She nodded, smiled, gave me a quick peck, and left the dining room.

****

When did our relationship go downhill? Was it during the computer crash when I was downsized twice and descended from Program Manager to insurance agent? Was it her burnout from Nursing that led her to re-train for cosmetology? Hell, I'm a good

19

insurance man and she's a genius with cosmetics, manicures, waxing, and hair styling. Whom am I kidding? We both had our dream careers; we both lost our dreams. We're coping; but with something hollow inside.

Where did the passion go? Maybe our carnal life never sizzled; but it was adequate. Somewhere along the way, we settled into our routine. But now we even stopped doing that. Did the abortion have something to do with it? I mean, come on! It was a mutual decision. We have three kids, a lot of bills, and shaky career platforms. Adrienne did not want another child at the age of forty, especially since the marriage was strained.

Why did she push my hand away at the table? Why did she see my whole speech as some kind of guilt trip?

I took a drink of water, made a pit stop, and then trudged into the TV room. We sat on the same couch, but with space between us. The canned laughter was taunting me. It was some kind of cosmic joke.

3

The Morning City

O nce again, I'm awake before the radio alarm. The shimmer of the Morning City is peeking through our blinds. Despite my "moonlighting", I lay in bed, fully awake, with a surge of cascading thoughts. Kenny's been giving me a lot of shit for not finalizing a couple of contracts. What am I supposed to, put a gun to their heads? More than anyone else in the office, he should know the complexity and ambivalence around insurance policies. Of course, Chuck is no help with his obnoxious jokes and provocations. He's learned to leave Sylvia alone. She'll go all 'ghetto' on his ass. I appreciate Harry, the philosopher, more and more. "They're just filling up the void in their lives," he'd tell me over lunch at the local bar. Then he jokes about Sylvia, our not-too-discreet divorcee. But Harry's jokes are never malicious; just pleasant notations about the absurdity of life. Why did Brin start to cry last night? She did assure me it was not my fault. But she would not elaborate any further.

The kids are just starting to stir. I heard Candi's iPhone jingle and her skulk into the bathroom. Glenn grunted an incomprehensible curse when she told him to wake up. With Amanda now in college, Candi has assumed the role of extra-responsible child, which Glenn does not appreciate.

I turn toward Adrienne and softly wrap my arm around her. Sabrina loves to "spoon". Not so Adrienne. With an angry snarl, she grabs my hand and shoves my arm away. "Stoppit!" A stab of hurt slashes through my gut and dissipates. I'm getting used to the rejections. Perhaps I should stop trying. Accept it. The limerance phase is long over, dude. But why such an angry reaction? She could just move my arm away. She can't still be tired; she went to sleep about ten.

With a sigh, I get up and stretch. After a quick bathroom stint, I get into my shorts and sneakers. It's time for the morning jog. I miss Mandy, who sometimes would jog with me. After the run, we'd talk as we cooled down. The girl was thoughtful and perceptive. One time, as we strolled back to the house, she actually said, "Why don't you just get a mistress, Dad?" I just looked at her and went silent. Later, back in the house, she apologized for intruding. I nodded and replied, "You're a smart young woman." She smiled and kissed my cheek. I'd rather not even think about experiences awaiting her in college. For an annoying number of times, as we packed her car, I said, "Be careful". Sensitive to my concerns, she patiently nodded with a smile. But she knew that I knew that she knew. Awkward.

I like our neighborhood. It's just diverse enough. The Korean couple is always out jogging before I am. By the time I finish my stretches and run a few blocks, they pass me and look like they just ran a marathon. With drenched shirts and frazzled hair, they greet me with a wave and a nod. The Spanish family nearby is always in a rush because of the ridiculous high school hours. It's a crime to make teenagers attend class so damn early. The Greek who owns the local diner probably sleeps less than I do. The family of the black doctor includes a few musicians and sweet jazz emanates from their barbecues. It's ironic that the all-American White family down the block seems the most detached. They're polite enough with a wave or a greeting, but that's it. I guess it's related to the flag in their window with one star.

Nice weather today, comfortably warm, low humidity, and a pleasant breeze. It's in contrast to last night when we actually put up the heat in the room. The season is turning. That means the darkness will come sooner so Sabrina may start work earlier.

Why did she cry last night? I re-ran the tape in my head. I made a few bitter jokes about co-workers and she talked about some of the other girls. Coo went overboard with makeup while Tabby hated everyone. We laughed a lot. Then she went silent and tears started to flow. When I noticed the reaction, Brin turned away from me and grabbed some tissues to wipe her face. Turning back to me, her eyes fluttered and she made an effort to smile.

I've grown to care a lot about her. "What is it?" I inquired. "Something I said?" The change was so sudden that I assumed I must have hit a button.

"No, of course not," she answered. "It's not always about you." Her reply was sharp, critical. I was puzzled. But she soon bounced back. "I'm sorry, you didn't deserve that." She gave me a quick peck and rubbed my neck. I put my forehead against her's. We sat that way for a while, with our heads together, and silently absorbed the mood. She whispered something with the word "consensual" in it. Perhaps we'll re-visit the issue at another time.

By the time I got back to the house, eggs were cooking, coffee was brewing, and the kids were texting. The smells of breakfast provoked my stomach to complain. So I hydrated and threw two more eggs on the grill. Adrienne didn't have to be at the salon until noon, a far cry from her crazy hours when she was nurse. She hit her forties and decided cosmetology was more to her liking. The kids used to tease her and call it cosmology. Wise-guy Glenn kept promising to buy her a telescope. I read a few articles and warned her about DBP, formaldehyde, and other toxins. Adrienne became indignant and reminded me that, as a nurse, she had dealt with worse things. I can only imagine! Nonetheless, her hours doing manicures, pedicures, waxings, cosmetics, and massages were more convenient for the family. I used to wonder why I never got a massage. She would sarcastically say she separates her work from her family life. Indeed! By comparison, Sabrina gives a wonderful massage, deep and penetrating; and she enjoys doing it for me. It never feels like a chore when Brin and I give to each other; it's always a playful pleasure. After the demands of her work, you'd think she would resent having to service any man any further. But it's just the opposite. "The rest is just rehearsal," she would say. Oh my god!

The kids caught the school bus and we both finished our coffee, and Adrienne supplied a gentle reminder. "You did cancel your night job, right?" I looked up from my cup. "For Glenn, Barry. Meet the Teachers." Oh shit! I forgot.

"Why didn't you remind me sooner?" I demanded.

She stared into her own cup. "I did," she retorted. "All week."

"Oh yeah." I was nailed. "I'll make a few calls, to see if someone else can cover for me."

Adrienne slammed her cup down and pushed her chair away from the table. "Really? You kidding me?" She brought her dishes to the sink and scrubbed off the egg residue with excessive force. "You just don't give a damn, do you?" It wasn't a question but an indictment.

I had nothing left but to counter-attack. "Give it a break, will you? I'm working two jobs for this family."

"Right, the perfect family guy!"

I finished my coffee and dropped the cup in the sink. "I have to get to work. You know? The first job? Don't worry, I'll handle it." I didn't want to leave that way so I turned and approached her. "Adrienne, honey…"

"Stop. Just go!" Wonderful! Two attempts and two rejections in one morning!

It was the constant rejections, the hostility, and her current chastity that led me into the arms of another. But the shadow relationship is distracting. I forget what Adrienne tells me; bring home the wrong items from the supermarket; overlook scheduled events; miss cues in conversations. She accuses me of not caring. The truth is I care too much about all the players in my life.

****

The agency of Huntington Insurance is a modest affair. Kenny had his own office in the rear. He was enclosed in glass walls, the better to spy on his subordinates. The serfs had their separate cubicles. Each of us did what we could to humanize and individualize our bit of space that was surrounded by moveable panels. Any reductions in staff were easily accommodated. At least the panels were tackable, so we could display paintings, photographs, cartoons, drawings our kids made, and relevant news articles. Of course, any awards for productivity achievements were top priority. When Sylvia was out sick, we didn't have a receptionist. Any agent could pass on messages from clients.

It was fun to take on a new customer, sort of like recruiting a convert to your little cult. But once the newbies were processed, the job was pretty mindless. Customers came in to pay premiums or get some clarification on their policies. Questions were answered on the phone. Kenny spent a lot of time reading newspapers and planning his next vacation. The serfs keep up enough activity to keep Kenny happy. Most of the time, when I checked the computer screen for client activity, I thought back to how I used to program those damn databases. Most of the time, as a programmer, you didn't care about the content; you were engaged in the creative process of organizing the raw data into manageable components and allowing any user to present a professional report. Now, at the level of content, it was mind numbing. But it was perfect for my additional activities.

What asshole came up with the idea of incentives? I hate the dog-treat rationale behind it. With enough productivity, you win a weekend at the Marriott. The really super-duper champions get to attend the annual Convention. Rumor has it that it's an opportunity to meet some prime hookers. Really? Do tell! The company picks up the tab for your room and your food. Hookers and drinks are your responsibility. So the suckers return broke any way. I prefer to continue under the radar, performing at my moderate but acceptable rate, and choose my fun on my own time.

Finally, she called me back. "Hey, Barry. It's early for me."

"Brin, I have a family issue tonight." From his fishbowl, Kenny is observing me on my personal phone.

"Oh." She was silent for a long time; not a good sign. "I have a big customer tonight," she reminded me. "It's political."

"Baby, we both have family values, right?" She concurred. "It's Meet-The-Teacher Night at my son's junior high school. If I don't go…"

"Yeah. I get it. If I take a cab, can you be there later?"

"Cool. I'll tell Adrienne that I had limited coverage. It'll probably be over by eight."

"Ok. But, Barry, I need you there when I'm done." She sounded more anxious than usual. "They have to know you're waiting for me."

I was taken aback. "They?" Sounds like an adventurous evening.

My question seemed to irk her. "The less you know, the better for you." Very clear, very precise, very conclusive.

"Wow. Ok. I'll be there by ten." She gave me the address, which I jotted down quickly. I made sure I could read my own scribble. She verified it. I folded the paper and slipped it in my wallet.

Kenny was flexible about personal calls during work hours, as long as you got the job done. He saw the paper action. As soon as I hung up on Brin, he called me. "Everything OK, Barrett?"

"Yeah, no problem. Family stuff. A teachers meeting tonight."

"Your kid in trouble?" He had a tendency to probe.

"No, boss. The usual meet-and-greet."

"Oh, that thing," he replied. "Pretty useless if you ask me." I didn't.

"Well, it's useful if they meet you in person, ya know, in case anything does come up."

How can a sniff be condescending? He managed it. "If you think so," he concluded. "I got a message from Mrs. Parker, the widow. She wants to know about her fire coverage."

"No problem. I'm on it." That lonely widow calls me five times every week. But that's OK. I get it. Loneliness.

****

At my lunch break, I headed to the diner. My Greek neighbors were the owners and they were generous with dessert. I sat down and put in my order. As the waitress left, I opened my wallet and took out the paper. I typed the address and the time in my phone calendar, double-checked it, hit the save button, and put the phone back in its pouch. The waitress arrived more quickly than usual and I was startled as the tray landed on the table. "Very efficient!" I quipped and she gave me a wink. Her name was Judy; a grad student with plans to be a lawyer. Smart girl.

While I bit into my turkey sandwich, Harry the philosopher appeared at my table. We gave each other a nod. But Harry had something to say. He sat at my booth. He tapped the table in a restive state and seemed jittery about a covert message.

"You alright?" I maundered between bites.

With a deep sigh, he took the plunge. "The walls of the cubicles aren't sound-proof," he declared. "You're lucky that I'm your neighbor. Chuck is a loudmouth and Tanya resents everybody." I was eager to provide an alibi but he waved me off. "Don't sweat, man. I have my own skeletons. In fact…" He paused to sip some water and look around the diner. "I just lost my own special friend. Comprendez? She vanished, man!"

"Hmm. Too bad." What else could I say?

"I have no idea what happened to her." He looked genuinely sad. "I mean, I'm not stupid. I get the arrangement. But, over time, it really did feel like something real." His finger slid across the rim of the glass. "What happens to a woman like that? Do they just find a better city? Ah!" He shrugged. "I just sharing this to say you can trust me."

"Cool."

"Did you use the Internet?" I shook my head. "So it was a traditional meeting. Nice. Let me know if she has any friends, ok?"

"No problem." So Harry and I now shared a bond of secrecy. What happens to women like that, he asked. I think I know but I kept it to myself. Sabrina shared some bad stories with me. Because of that, I wanted more information. "Hey, Harry, this friend?" He glanced at me with raised eyebrows. "Just curious. What was her nationality?"

He scrutinized my face and decided it was OK. "Some place in Asia. I looked it up. Uzbekistan. Why'd you ask?"

I had learned a lot with Sabrina as a good teacher. Talking almost to myself, I mumbled, "Yeah. Significant slave labor." Then I looked at Harry. "Was she freelancing?"

"You're kidding me!" he replied sarcastically. "I never got a dossier on her."

4

The First Encounter

I t's an obvious plot. The robots are not only conscious of themselves but of their situation. A rebellion is building. It's not a bad book.

Sabrina and I were together before her work tonight. Adrienne was busy at the salon and the kids were in school. We arranged an afternoon together. It was wonderful. I brought bagels and she brewed coffee. We listened to classical music on her phone and we had hours to play. After our hours of pure joy, we washed each other diligently and sensually in the hot shower. I loved to go down on her while she was moist from the stream. She used soap elegantly all over me. Frothy hands enrich the sensation. We embraced under the cascade for our own personal eternity. We were no longer in a merchant/customer relationship; but calling her my mistress just didn't seem to jive. Lovers? That didn't quite fit either. Whatever we had, it was special. Small wonder I forgot about Meet-The-Teacher.

Tonight, she entertained a newbie in a safe hotel and I tried to concentrate on my book. But memories of our first encounter sent me into a pleasant dream. I let the river of reflection flow freely.

When you have enough of bourgeois gentility, there's always Nobody's Bar at the lower end of a street in Chelsea, just far enough away from the Highline to avoid tourists with their incessant cameras. It was a hole in the wall that was easy to miss but well known to locals. No fancy marquee attracted tourists. There were no microbrewery specials; just your regular beers, the ones your father used to drink. It was also home base for women of a certain persuasion.

I should've checked my horoscope that morning. Some rogue planet was controlling events. Adrienne was nasty on the phone as she complained about a chore I had forgotten. Glenn needed more notebooks from a popular discount store, near my job. When I rushed out of the house that morning to catch the train, I agreed to pick them up during lunch. But then the day got away from me. Kenny was in a foul mood and monthly stats were due. Sylvia's son was sick so the agents had to cover the receptionist duties as well as their own. Chuck got a little too loud during lunch. He was giving the waitress a hard time and I told him to calm down, which only riled him up further. So we got into an argument and Chuck implied that I was turned on by the girl. I apologized to the waitress for my colleague's behavior and then left the restaurant. Still rattled, I took a brisk walk to shake off the emotional residue, browsed a few newspaper headlines, and jaunted back to the office. Chuck later apologized and we shook hands but the stress lingered. The poor guy is jumping hoops to win that trip to the Convention. Why doesn't the stupid peasant just purchase a plane ticket and rent a room there? Oh yeah, land of the free!

When Adrienne scolded me, it tipped my scales. I barked at her, hung up the phone and decided I needed a drink; or at least some refuge from the madness of modern life. The waitresses at Nobody's would never cave in to Chuck's harassment. They were cute but tough. The repartee was often playfully hostile. Renee, the Italian single Mom from Astoria, welcomed me in her typical style. "Oh, shit! Another stray dog from the alley."

"Yeah, love you too," I replied with a sneer.

With hands on her hips, she said, "You want a beer or you gonna keep me waiting? I'm busy, you know."

"You're supposed to wait," I answered. "You're a waitress." She snickered as I scanned the bar and counted three customers sipping their drinks. "Yeah, I see. The place is jumpin'." I ordered a stout beer from the tap and some peanuts. With a little effort, I managed to focus on a soccer game playing on the large TV. For a while, I disappeared in a dark corner.

I was absorbed in the action on the screen and didn't notice her right away. "May I join you?"

The soft sound of her voice stirred me awake. She's about my height, maybe an inch shorter. I remember the first time I noticed her jet-black hair that fell to her waist but had an easy flow when she moved her head. Her figure was perfect, slender but not skinny. She wore a short violet skirt of some kind of spandex, revealing slender but strong legs. Her dark eyes have an Asian slant that she augmented with kohl and eye shadow. Adrienne had taught me a lot about cosmetic tricks, but this woman knew how to apply makeup with a professional flair. In the dim light, her skin had a copper glow that fascinated me. Her subtle lips were shaped into an irresistible pout.

She raised her eyebrows and waited for my reply. Her posture was more of a demand than a request. Struggling to catch my breath, I stammered out, "Of course. I could use the company." She slinked into the chair with serpentine command.

"My name is Sabrina," she told me before I thought to ask.

"Barrett," I replied in turn. "Would you care for a drink?" I couldn't believe this was happening to me.

"Perhaps some wine. I like Chianti."

I turned to summon the waitress and discovered that Renee was already there, with her pad out, ready to take an order. I ordered Sabrina's Chianti and Sabrina suggested some bread for the table as well. Renee seemed to snicker and walked to the bar.

Sabrina offered an explanation. "Renee knows me. This is a regular stop for me." She looked up at the TV. "Do you like soccer?"

I was glad that Sabrina was leading the conversation. "Sometimes," I said. I tried to guess her ethnicity but was at a loss. "Do they enjoy soccer a lot in your country?"

Sabrina laughed gently. "You mean the country of Manhattan, New York, USA?"

I felt the flush rise in his face. "I'm sorry," I said like the awkward boob I was. "I foolishly assumed…"

"Perhaps I'm an illegal alien, an exotic spy." She leaned in closer. "An international jewel thief. You think so?"

I started to regain my poise. "That covers most of the usual movie plots. Again, I apologize." I raised my forearms, rested my chin on my hands, and stared at her with growing curiosity.

She reached across the table and stroked my arm. "Actually, I'm what you're searching for." I'll never forget that line! Her dark hair fell between us. My arms went numb as I resisted the impulse to sweep my hands through those strands.

A question formed in my mouth but I swallowed it back down. I preferred silence and waited for the intriguing woman to elaborate.

Renee broke the silence. "As ordered. One Chianti and some bread. I took the liberty to add butter. Want another beer?"

"No thanks, I'm good," I answered.

Renee wrote out the check and dropped it on the table. "Good idea," she said. "Stay alert." Sabrina glared at her. Renee winked and left us alone.

I tried to decipher the words of the waitress. Sabrina spoke. "Do you have somewhere to go?"

With a smirk, I answered, "Not right away."

Sabrina tilted her head. Her hair fell across her face. She was analyzing a subject. "You're married, aren't you?" Somehow she concluded that from my pained expression.

Reluctantly, I nodded and felt like a guilty sinner in a confession box. I expected our conversation to end at that.

"So anything we do would have to be just for the moment." Again, I chose silence and patience. "How much do you want me?"

I was surprised by her bluntness. But her question was ambiguous.

"I'm not sure I understand."

Sabrina studied me. "I don't think you're a cop." I laughed and shook my head. "Of course not." She slowly sipped her Chianti, then put down the glass and ran her finger along its rim. In a near-whisper, she asked, "How much would you pay me? What am I worth?" Another question that will be with me forever.

I was enlightened. "Of course. For a moment, I thought you were really attracted to me."

"I am attracted to you," she countered. "I never invite someone I don't like." I gazed at her, searching for the truth. Then I checked my phone. "Your wife, did she text you?"

I quickly shut the phone and put it away. "We had an argument. I told her I needed some time. So, no, she didn't text."

"How much time, Barrett?"

I paused for a minute to comprehend the question. I tried to calculate all the possible ramifications. Then the words just came out of my mouth. "I really want to do this." My heart was pounding and blood was pumping through my chest and face. I could feel the heat.

"Will you come to my room?" She was calm and clear.

I'm usually a cautious guy; but then I veered into paranoia. "Is that when the pimp comes out and kills me?" Although I tried to make it sound like a joke, the fear was real.

Sabrina pursed her lips and frowned. If she was acting offended, she was doing a good job. "I'm an independent," she answered. "I've dealt with a few pimps; but I like my freedom. Ever since high school. I don't intrude on them and they don't bother me."

"I just met you. How do I know I can trust you?"

"Barrett, you're about to miss an opportunity and you'll always regret it." She pointed her thumb back to Renee. "Do you think she's helping me pile up all the bodies? Really?" I noticed her long fingernails, painted purple. She sipped the libation slowly, closed her eyes, and rolled her head backward while the sensation flowed within her. I desperately wanted her to react to me like that.

She finished her Chianti, took a piece of bread, stood up and extended her arm to me. "Come," she said as she nibbled the bread. What a scene! I paid the bill, took her hand and stood up. I nervously grabbed a slice of bread as we left the bar.

Thoughts were crashing and colliding in my head. After the evening with Adrienne, I wanted to rebel, to regress into some primordial stage from my younger days. What happened to

Adrienne? Everything I enjoy she despises: the city, the park, the cafes, the music. Whatever I tried to share was rejected. Why did she really quit nursing? Did she grow tired of caring for vulnerable people? Did hospital politics leave her so bitter that she abandoned the vocation? Cosmetology is still a type of caretaking; but it enhances beauty. Perhaps she grew wary of the ugly medical realities of life. That would fit with her sudden burst of spirituality. So maybe it has to do with trauma; too many fatalities, too many frantic parents, too many ruined lives.

There is another kind of caretaking. When Sabrina approached me, I was as vulnerable as a patient on a gurney in the E.R. Her dark silken hair and her golden copper skin entranced me. I wanted to touch that skin, to sink into its softness. Her dark eyes were like magnets and I was a pile of helpless iron filings. Her smile transmitted awareness of my hunger.

There was no question that I had gone for the bait. She held my hand and took me outside where the late-night air chilled my skin. But my shivering had several causes. She hailed a cab and I followed her like an obedient child. During the short ride, Sabrina stroked both my thighs and had no qualms about making contact with the region between them. Her subtle sweeps were like magic, more amorous than lewd. Lost sensations were re-awakening.

The hotel clerk knew her well and they exchanged casual greetings with smiles and waves. We entered an elevator and ascended to the fourth floor. Walking down the hallway, I began to feel disoriented. The mixture of beer, this sudden change in venue, and this amazingly exotic woman was having its effect.

The hotel room was modest but sufficient. The main light switch had a dimmer and Sabrina set it to a soft atmosphere, just enough to render her skin an iridescent gold. She shut the door and we stood close to each other. At the same time, I wanted to both ravish her and worship her. I put my hands around the back of her head and moved her face closer to me. For the first time, I realized she had beads in her hair. The beads clicked as my hands disturbed her strands. To my surprise, she did not resist my kissing her. Most professionals tend to avoid kissing. Perhaps we gauged each other as

34

hygienic enough. The kissing was sustained, mutually satisfying, wet and welcoming.

While we kissed, she unfastened my belt and opened my pants. I let them fall to the floor while she played with me over my underwear. I wanted to go slowly but passion was increasing rapidly. I stepped out of the pants as she pushed me towards the bed. "Lie down," she commanded. "Watch me."

She slithered out of the skirt and kept her eyes fastened upon me as she removed her blouse. The bra was one of those skimpy things that she discarded readily. Her breasts were a comfortable size, a healthy handful, and her nipples were taut within modest aureoles. Like the rest of her, the nipples were copper. She slipped out of her panties like a viper coming in for the kill. Her slender hips swiveled around a tight waist. She had shaved but not excessively.

Kneeling next to me, Sabrina let her breasts stroke my chest. I let my hands wander wherever they chose as she pulled off my underwear. Her skin was even softer than I had expected, like combed velvet. Moving her face to my penis, she blew air gently at it. Waves of passion were rushing up and down my spine. I continued to run my fingers through her hair. Then she kissed it, a playful, loving compression of her lips against my shaft. I surrendered and laid back, gazed at her, and softly repeated her name. Sabrina. Sabrina.

She put me in her mouth and let her tongue swirl around me. I begged her, "Please. Now." She understood, rose, and mounted me. With ease, I entered her. Her body seemed to embrace me with her wet warmth. Our separate rhythms merged into one harmony, surging toward an inevitable climax. For that moment, any distinction between right and wrong was lost. If I were to die just then, my life would be complete.

I think we came together, but I'm not sure. After all, she is a professional and knows how to perform with authenticity. I'll always remember how she collapsed upon me, as if totally exhausted by the lovemaking. For a small eternity, we laid on the bed like that. Finally, she stirred.

"I have to use the bathroom," she murmured. Rising, she added, "Why don't you remove the bedspread? Let's use the blankets now." She gave me a quick peck and scurried off to the bathroom. In our lust, we did drop on the made bed. I also became aware that the air conditioning in the room was cool. It was time to use the blankets. But first, I also had to use the toilet. I peed while she washed her pudenda. Then she used the same washcloth to wipe me. Of course, that led to more kissing. With cleansed genitals, we returned to the bedroom. Sabrina turned the radio on to a jazz channel while I brewed a cup of coffee.

Listening to a good combo while we shared the cup of coffee, under the covers together, cozy and relaxed, life was good. It got even better when we engaged in a second round of glorious sex. We took our time, really enjoyed the rhythm of our undulations, and came with better intensity than the first time. That time, I was pretty certain we both reached the mountaintop.

I don't know when we actually fell asleep. I woke with Sabrina in my arms. She had none of Adrienne's hang-ups; she embraced me comfortably while she slept. I wanted to stop time.

****

The moments after good sex were beautiful. A blanket of calm enclosed us in a shroud that tuned out the rest of the world. Sabrina reclined comfortably, with eyes closed, as I stroked her arm with gentle sweeps. I ran my hand across her hip, which bore a kundalini tattoo. The serpent coiled around its base and then started its upward surge. Her skin was so soft that I imagined silk or velvet. Her pigmentation fascinated me. It defied easy description. She hated, "bronze", because it was over-used like a simplistic default. Golden copper? Café latte with a hint of rose? Olive? Amber? She liked the allusion to amber since it was a substance that preserved remnants from the past.

I tried to rephrase the question that backfired in the bar. "What is your ethnicity? Your heritage?" I asked leisurely. It was a question borne of innocent curiosity, with no trace of racist pollution. She slowly opened her eyes and gazed at me in a way that was piercing but not threatening, challenging but not hostile. The oriental slant of her eyes mesmerized me. "What do you think I am?" she inquired with a playful smirk.

"Hmm. You can't be Mexican, not with those eyes."

"No, senior," she replied with a gentle giggle. "Don't be so lazy. Try harder."

"Maybe you're from Brazil."

"Change your geography. Don't be so Eurocentric."

I took the hint. " Arabic? Turkish, maybe, or Iranian."

She pursed her lips into a pout. "You're in the general vicinity," she answered with a nod. "Selijuk."

I stopped the stroking. I crinkled my brow. "Seli-who?"

She sat up on the bed and crossed her legs. Taking my face in her hands, she leaned in close. "Think of Central Asia, Barrett Sherman." She had this thing about saying my whole name when she wanted to make a point or relish the moment with extra drama. It always worked. "Children of Genghis Kahn, nomads pouring down from the steppes. We left our mark in Persia, in Turkey, in Afghanistan. The Great Alexander knew about us." She ran her index finger down the side of my face. "Mostly forgotten, we left artifacts and influence throughout that region." She rose from the bed, stood next to me, and began to swivel her hips. Despite the drain of our recent sex, the undulation of her body, so close to me and concealed by a delicate sheet, began to arouse me once again. "I am your Salome," she murmured. "Your gypsy priestess, your Jezebel."

I put my hands on her hips and let the erotic sensation of her motions lured me back into her snare. I moved in and kissed her navel. Then my tongue traveled across her stomach. She crunched my hair in her clenched fists. "I'm the girl your mother warned you about." She respired with a sustained, "Aah".

"The Whore of Babylon," I murmured as my fingertips ran down her sides.

"That's the *Sacred* Whore, you barbarian," she corrected me with a gasp. "I'm the one the fanatic prophets would curse." She began to hum. "I'm the 'satanic verses'. The disobedient Lilith."

I pulled her down onto the bed and tore off her sheet. With her legs spread and bent to the floor, I devoured her. With my thumbs, I separated her lips and stroked her pleasure spot. I drank in her sacred juices like a man desperate with thirst.

Satiated, I stood up and entered her inner sanctum, her holy of holies, which responded lovingly, wrapping around my aroused member in a loving embrace. We were transcended. Time had no relevance in our eternity of deep intimacy. It didn't matter how many lovers she entertained; nor who she thought was the best of her lovers. Only the present moment was of any consequence. After prolonged thrusting and the inevitable eruption, I collapsed and stayed inside her for another eternity. Neither of us wanted to fracture the union we had created. Despite the sordid reality of her profession and our arrangement, we were two frightened, innocent children, clinging to each other for comfort and validation.

"Selijuk," I whispered, like a prayer. She responded with a deep inhalation and slipped into sleep. "Could I do this?" I wondered. "Fall asleep and stay inside her?"

****

I woke to Sabrina's whimpering and thrashing. At first, I stroked her forehead; then took hold of her shoulders. Still in the throes of the nightmare, she swung her head back and forth. "Brin, wake up!" I shouted to. "Brin!"

Still half asleep, she pushed me away and flailed her arms. I took hold of her wrists and spoke firmly. Finally, she emerged fully awake.

"Omygod!" she gasped. "What did I do?" She was dazed.

"You were crying and fighting in your sleep. You tried to hit me." Her pained expression stirred my compassion. "No, you didn't hurt me."

Sabrina moved closer and embraced me. We began to rock like babies in a cradle. "I couldn't fight them off," she whispered. "The bitch was shaving me. The man, the leader, kept calling me 'Squirrel', and laughed at my useless struggling. She cursed and told me to stop squirming. If she cut me, it would hurt more when we…" She paused to consider how much to reveal. "I've been through a lot, Barrett. I want you to know that. But they never broke me."

"Yeah, I get it. Take it easy. Just be here with me."

"I don't want to hate," she murmured. "I need you. I trust you. You're a good man, Barry." After a pause, she added, "Please don't betray me. When it's time for us to end it, just be honest."

"I hear you, baby." At that moment, she did feel like my baby; like a frightened child in need of my holding. "I don't think I'll ever end it with you." I regretted saying that. The arrangement couldn't continue forever. But the pure joy of our time together, the sacred innocence of it, kept me bound to her.

But, there is a reality beyond us. I'm married with children. She might just have something else on schedule. I slipped out of the bed and took a shower, washing off any blatant evidence. I started getting dressed when Sabrina woke.

"Do you have to go?" she asked with large eyes. The exotic creature of the night had transformed into a sad little girl.

I was surprised. "You actually want me to stay?"

She purred. "Like I said, I really do like you." Then she lowered her eyes. "Of course, you are married. I understand. But I want to make you an offer." Just like that, she offered me the job!

5

The Salon

With her hands in latex gloves, Adrienne scrubbed the inside of the pedicure basin and removed remnants from the last treatment. Her nursing experience was a benefit for her clients since she was very germ-conscious. Once the tub was visibly clean, she gave it an extra rinse with Mar-V-Cide and ran hot water. For some reason, watching the water drain in a swirl from the tub filled Adrienne with sadness. Pulling the gloves off her hands, she placed them in a sanitary dispenser and sat down.

All the remains of the day were plummeting into the singularity of water and gravity through a narrow drain; into the black hole of the unknown beyond her personal salon. Every detail of Adrienne's life was also descending into meaninglessness. Her time with Barrett wore the semblance of a skilled performance; but the play itself was approaching some final scene.

The conversation that day at the salon scratched a few nerves. Sitting with her head in the drying hood, Ruth, the doctor's wife, spoke of her plans for her thirtieth anniversary: a big gathering with her family. If her sisters and brothers spoke as non-stop as she did, the walls might rumble. Adrienne was at the tub, pumicing the feet of Margaret, the elderly Irish widow, when Tabitha entered the salon. Tabitha, 28, is a slender attractive black woman who recently announced her engagement. She didn't flaunt a large stone, as Ruth would have done; such "symbols of bondage" did not appeal to her. Ruth gave a grunt at the remark. Tab and Gregory were thinking about a simple ceremony; maybe they'd elope to Las Vegas or New Orleans or Aruba. As the conversation proceeded, Margaret smiled or nodded her head, choosing to be an observant listener rather than an active participant.

"Spend a fortune on an obsolete ritual," Tabitha rumbled as she swept aside her hair extensions. "Put my folks in debt for some ego trip. It's foolish."

"I remember my wedding," replied Ruth in a nostalgic mode. "I remember the look on Harold's face while my father walked me to the bimah. He was so happy and wore a beautiful suit." Her fingers wiped first her eyes; then her ring. "So many of the people who were there I miss," she added with a sigh. "The 'obsolete ritual' filled me with a memory forever." Margaret, at the tub, laughed quietly and nodded.

"I guess that's nice enough," said Tabitha. "But here's the memory I'll have instead. A few days in New Orleans, or maybe a Caribbean island, stayin' in bed as long as we like and doin' whatever we like. Maybe we find an isolated cove and make love in a cave by the beach. How about dancing, maybe reggae, to steel drums on a hot night, drinking pina coladas, and grinding on the dance floor at 3am? And saving the family a whole lot of money at the same time." Ruth growled and Margaret laughed a little louder.

"Whatever," replied Ruth, feeling defeated but remaining proud. "I can only hope you'll make it to thirty years."

"What?" asked Tabitha. "A wedding ritual is gonna get me thirty years of marital bliss? Hell, after a couple of months, you won't even know where the wedding album is! And you won't care either." Then she became more subdued. "Besides, there are no guarantees. I have my doubts about the whole thing. I mean, you know, Greg and I are doing fine. Why mess it up?" From the tub, Margaret let out a low hum.

"So marriage messes every thing up, eh?" Ruth patted her perm to check its hold. "Where's the romance? Where's the caring? The sharing?" Margaret shook her head and kept silent.

"You don't think we care and share? Why not? Because we like to drink and turn each other on and get crazy sometimes?" Adrienne and Margaret both giggled. "It's not either/or, Ruth. In fact, it better be both."

Adrienne wiped her hands while Margaret relaxed with closed eyes. Adrienne went to Ruth, turned off the hood and moved it away from her.

"So what do you think?" asked Ruth. "A nice wedding or a hedonistic escape?"

Adrienne pondered the question. She could feel Tabitha's eyes on her. Ruth sat gazing into the mirror. "There's no right or wrong way," she finally replied. "People do what they feel is right for them."

"Sure," countered Ruth. "But which way means more in the end?"

"I don't know," answered Adrienne, as her fingers anxiously combed through Ruth's perm, and adjusted hairpins. "No marriage is perfect. We all go through difficult…"

Adrienne was interrupted by the jingle of the bell on the entrance door. Sarita, a sparkly 20-year-old Latina, sashayed into the salon. She wore a short skirt that amply revealed shapely legs, to the envy of older patrons. Her dark brown hair fell beyond her shoulders in a soft wave. Her long fingernails glimmered with the latest acrylics. "Hey, girls," she called out while chewing gum. "Hey, Adrienne! You busy?"

"Hi, Sari. I'm just finishing up with Ruth, and Margaret is pretty much done. I have one appointment coming in. So I'll get to you in about fifteen minutes, OK?"

"No prob." Sarita scanned the salon walls. "I'll check out the nail colors. Coffee?"

"Sure, have some." Adrienne had a pod machine that her clients were free to use.

Sarita made her selection, popped in a pod, and pushed the button. "I'm goin' out tonight with a new guy. I like him a lot. I wanna make him forget all the other girls." Tabitha laughed. Margaret woke from her nap and smiled readily when she noticed Sarita. Ruth pursed her lips but continued to stare into the mirror.

"Hey, girl," exclaimed Tabitha. "You're already a hottie. You don't have to improve anything."

Sarita leaned into Tabitha. "There's always room to improve," she answered and they laughed with conspiratorial glee.

"Naughty girl," declared Tabitha.

"Takes one to know one," countered Sarita.

Margaret pulled her legs from the basin and wiped her feet. "I loved that time in my life," she said to the two collaborators. "I wish it could last forever."

"Peggy, you don't sound like an old Irish lady," Sarita noted as she played with several nail polish jars.

"You think you invented sex?" asked Margaret with a grumble. "Yeah, I was raised god-fearin' church-going Irish. We hung up curtains. But, you know, when people think you're a 'good girl', they don't watch you so much."

"All right!" exclaimed Tabitha with a laugh. She and Sarita high-fived. "How long were you married, Peggy?"

After a pause, Margaret asked in return, "Which time?" They were surprised. "I was married three times, and had a few other lovers along the way."

Adrienne's jaw dropped. Ruth's expression bordered on pain. Tabitha let loose with, "Damn!" Sarita exclaimed, "Mazel tov!"

Ruth thanked Adrienne for a good perm, paid the fee, and added a decent tip. "I guess we all make our own choices," she declared. "Good luck and be careful." She left the salon with a friendly wave.

****

Adrienne shut the music and sat on the stool, in quiet contemplation, away from scissors and bobby pins, acrylics and nail clippers, moisturizers and gels, shampoos and conditioners. The little whirlpool in the basin focused her attention. There's never enough quiet time in the modern world. Even when people have to wait in a line for five minutes, they zip out their cell phones. We seek distraction; but from what? The mini-maelstrom served as a moving mandala, forcing her into reflection. It was all rushing down the drain. Mandy was in college now, pursuing her own dreams. Candi was confronting the challenges of adolescence with the typical mask of arrogant defiance. Glenn had his homework, his sports, and his iPhone. A phase was slipping away from her; Adrienne was left with a sense of obsolescence, like a phonograph in our digital age. She was plummeting in a whirlwind. Like a passenger of an amusement park ride, centripetal forces pushed at her. She felt a bit dizzy.

And then there was Barrett. He took on a second job, a night shift. Moonlighting to bring in extra money, he explained. He was also avoiding the whirlpool, keeping busy, staying productive; to reassure himself that he still was relevant in the world. He was the good provider, paying for college costs and other household necessities. How could Adrienne complain about that? And yet she wanted desperately to complain, about something. Some indefinable agitation, it was a mixture of impatience, annoyance, sadness, and remorse. It would be easy to provoke an argument. They would both get to release some pent-up energy and have an excuse to leave each other alone. But the feeling would only build again. Is that how it was going to be: living from one uproar to the next? With no clear warning or signal, tears began to emerge. Adrienne just let them stream while she searched in the void for some meaning.

That was when the bell jingled. Sarita entered the darkened, silent salon and found Adrienne sitting on the stool near the pedicure tub. Adrienne quickly wiped her face, turned to Sarita, and made a sincere effort to smile. With her young body, skillfully applied makeup, and incessant gum chewing, the girl reflected a look of excited potential.

"With all our talking, I forgot the nail polish," Sarita announced with a nervous laugh. Then she noticed Adrienne's expression and the moisture in her eyes. "Are you OK?"

Adrienne tried to make a joke out of everything. "I think the conversation we had pressed some buttons," she explained. She grabbed some tissues and wiped her face.

"Yeah. Me too," replied Sarita.

Adrienne was surprised. "What do you mean? How…"

"Don't let my war paint fool you," Sarita disclosed. "You're a beautician. You know how it goes. A lot can be hidden away." Sarita sat on the shampoo chair. Adrienne stood, left the stool, and went to the barber chair. "Sometimes I envy women like Peggy. I mean, hell, she's in her eighties but she seems satisfied with her life, ya know?"

Adrienne snickered. "I had no idea how…er…active, her life was. Wow! Three husbands, lovers."

"Yeah. I had her figured as a typical old Irish-Catholic lady, all stiff-necked and judgmental. It just goes to show you."

"You're Catholic, right?" asked Adrienne. "I mean, you being Spanish."

"Hah! I'm more complicated than that. My father was casual Jewish but my mother was Catholic in a way."

"In a way?"

"She didn't do church every Sunday or anything like that. But, whenever she passed a church, she'd cross herself. My padre was pretty liberal about things; but mia madre was fiercely anti-abortion and often scolded me about sin. One time, when I argued with a nun in school, Dad cheered and Mom was horrified. They had to go to school. Mom apologized to the nun for me; but Dad challenged her authority. He said something like, 'School should be for expanding your mind; not obeying dogma.' Wow! That was cool. Needless to say, my parents had a hell of a fight when they got back home. They told me to keep out of it. But, hey, it was all about me!" Sarita laughed at the irony.

"So did you attend church or synagogue?"

"Dad sort of gave in on that," she explained. "He didn't care. So we did the big holy days, ya know? Christmas Mass, Easter."

"What about their wedding?" asked Adrienne.

"Unitarian Universalist," replied Sarita. They both laughed. It was a welcome relief. Between gasps, Sarita added, "Both families were angry about that!"

"Well, Thomas Jefferson would've liked it," declared Adrienne.

When their laughter fizzled out, Adrienne re-focused. "So the 'war paint', what's it hiding?"

Sarita grew quiet. Her smile went flat. She looked down. Her voice was lower than usual. She tossed her gum into the wastebasket. "It's a lot of competition, ya know? You may not want to, but you have to be an object. I have to attract guys, play with them, seduce them, before the other girl gets there first. You have to do it or you never get noticed. But then I'm just an object; they can toss me away easily."

"Hmm. A Catch-22," noted Adrienne.

Sarita looked puzzled. "What do you mean?" she inquired.

Adrienne was reminded about their age difference. "An old expression," she answered. "Like a double-bind."

"Yeah." It became silent enough for them to hear the last gurgle of water in the basin. "Maybe there's a reason I forgot the nail polish before," Sarita pondered. "Maybe I want to lose it all."

Sabotaging her own profession, Adrienne offered some advice. "What if you were just yourself? What if you did your own thing, followed your own path? Let the guys come to you. Then you'd know they cared about you; not just the mask or the hair or the figure. Right?"

"Hmm." Sarita nodded and considered the idea. "It could be a long wait," she countered. "They'd all be at the club dancing with one of the beauty queens."

"You are an interesting combination," observed Adrienne. "Pardon me in advance for the stereotypes. Your Spanish side wants to be flamboyant and sensual. Your Jewish side wants to ponder the meaning of life."

Sarita stared at her. "I'll try to forgive you for that," she replied. "Some of my Jewish relatives are real jerks; and some of the Spanish guys could pass as rabbis." Adrienne went palms up to beseech her forgiveness. "But you may be on to something. We all want to dance, sing, party, seduce. But we also want a serious relationship. We're at war with ourselves." Then Sarita turned the tables. "What about you? Why did you look so unhappy when I came in?"

Adrienne grunted. "Hmm. I did avoid that, eh?" Then she tried to explain. "There comes a time when all your investments don't seem so important any more. Making sure the kids get to the right college. Demanding that the coach lets your kid play. Getting all your charts in order. Playing the game to get promoted. Buying just the right dress. Having dinner with the right people at the right restaurant and ordering the right wine. It all just starts to feel so…"

"Meaningless?"

"More than that," replied Adrienne. "Absurd." Then she added, "The movie comedies? Maybe they have more truth than documentaries."

"Wow, that's deep!" Sarita's eyes were wide with wonder.

"You're so much younger than I am," Adrienne asserted.

"You make that sound like an insult," Sarita parried. Again Adrienne gestured for forgiveness. "And yet, it's the same issue for both of us." Adrienne crinkled her forehead in confusion so Sarita clarified. "We go out of our way to impress others; and then realize how foolish it is."

"Oh my god!" Adrienne was astonished. "You're right!"

"See," announced Sarita in triumph. "I'm smarter than I look!"

"C'mon," pleaded Adrienne. "I never meant anything like that and you know it. Maybe I wasn't p.c. enough but I was trying to be honest."

"I know," replied Sarita with a wave. "No prob. Besides, there's nothing some good sex won't tranquilize." Adrienne was startled by that quick segue and lowered her head. "Sometimes being a sex object ain't so bad." She chuckled and anticipated Adrienne's communal consent.

"Yeah," replied Adrienne with forced mutuality. "Right."

6

The Anniversary & The Disappearance

I guess it's a useful tradition. At least parents and teachers might recognize each other on school grounds. But, I must admit, little of what was said in each classroom was retained. I had a little notepad and wrote at least one comment in each classroom. I planned to impress Glenn with my interest in his school. Even that seemed to bother Adrienne. "You're taking notes during Meet The Teacher? Really?" I was suspecting that Adrienne just needed to vent her chagrin over life itself rather than actually being annoyed at me.

The Chemistry teacher seemed to know his stuff; but does that transfer to teaching abilities? Can he make Chem fun and comprehensible in junior high? Or does his expertise intimidate and baffle the students? The History teacher was cute in a recent-grad-student sort of way: glad to have a secure job with benefits and eager to enlighten her students about kings and queens, wars and martyrs, tyrants and reformers, revolutionaries and reactionaries. Good luck, girl! Would she be interested in the global economics I've learned from Sabrina? It would make a wonderful PhD thesis. I doubt it. She'll meet a colleague, fall in love, get married and struggle to get her own kids into a good school. I hope the Geometry teacher has adequate patience. The Gym teacher—make that Phys Ed---broke the stereotype of a muscle-bound knucklehead. He was slender but well built with endorphin-alert eyes. Compared to him, I immediately felt just as inadequate as the 12-year-old I used to be. But, hey, I had an ace in the hole. This smooth jock doesn't have Sabrina; unless he can afford her of course. Were teachers' salaries that good?

Between and during classroom visits, I kept checking my watch. Adrienne got annoyed. "Can't you just focus on your son for once?" she asked with legitimate pique.

"You're right. Sorry, hon." Even though Brin had a competent history before me, I didn't like her being unprotected. She had said the customer was "political" with "unique preferences". He was clearly a high status repeater client since she took him to her actual apartment. And what did she mean by "They"? Do I really want to know? So far, my phone did not vibrate but that was little consolation.

Every one was heading to the parking lot and school lights were switching off. "This night work isn't paying you enough," she grumbled as we headed to our separate cars. "The cost is too high."

"Yeah, right," I retorted. "Remember that when the car loan gets paid up and we take our cruise."

"That's all you care about, isn't it?" She always got the last word. I was tempted to escalate the argument but that would only waste more time.

"The stress of living in middle America," I concluded. "Can't be helped. I'll try to get back soon." She recognized the brush-off and gave a short grunt.

When I got in my own car, I connected my phone to the charger and made a quick check for messages or voice mails. Nothing. Traffic was light and I parked the car next to a fire hydrant, the space I considered my reserved spot. I scanned her apartment building. She lived on the second floor of a walkup in the lower twenties on the West Side. There was no doorman but the main entrance was always locked and you had to be buzzed in. Sabrina had supplied me with keys to her front entrance and her apartment. Her bedroom was lit with low-amps. It seemed copacetic enough so I flipped through my notepad and made sure I could decipher my own scribbles. Satisfied that Glenn would be impressed, I tossed the pad on the passenger seat and picked up the novel I was reading. With these late-night sojourns, I could qualify for a degree in literature.

To my surprise, Sabrina arrives while I was reading. Sabrina's young client looks toward me as I sit in the car. He gives me a quick nod and a smile. This young buck is her "political" customer? Probably the son of some wealthy politician. Just behind him is a slender figure in a hooded jacket. The three accomplices scurry into the building. Sabrina makes no gesture toward me as she leads the way. So it's come to this: I'm a driver for an exotic hooker whose adventurous clients are on friendly terms with me. If this scenario were a computer program, I'd be lost in a dysfunctional sub-program with a missing end-code. She was right about one thing: I'm surrendering possessiveness. Although I have strong feelings for her, I don't mind that she's getting very personal with another man and his covert companion. In fact, he and I probably could become friends. We could share a few drinks and laugh at each other's jokes. So I may not be a pimp; but I'm probably a cuckold.

As she and her clients disappear into her apartment building, I take my book light out of the glove compartment. Let's see, where was I? Oh yeah. The robots are developing some human consciousness. They're still subservient to their Makers; but they're evolving.

****

I remember the day so well, when I made my existential decision. When I woke that morning, I had devised an optimistic plan. Our 20-year anniversary was approaching; it was time for renewal. It was Monday, her day off from the salon. Our two girls were self-sufficient and Glenn only needed a bowl of cereal. The Buddhist meditations were having an impact: Compassion, radical acceptance, forgiveness, detachment. I was determined to change the path of my karma. I would forgive Adrienne for her limitations, accept her reality as well as my own, detach from negative emotions, and, with great compassion, display my love for her.

As she lay in bed, on her back, I turned to stroke her hair ever so gently. I thought the gesture was having the desired effect until she groaned and growled at me to stop "bothering" her. With loving determination, I pressed on, and wrapped my arm across her waist. With a sigh, she pushed my arm off and turned away from me. My Buddha-nature was facing a strong challenge! It was time for great compassion. With deep breaths, I inhaled the love of the universe and accepted the negative pattern we had developed over time. With profound optimism, I recognized that life is change. I would meet her negative energy with positive energy. We could alter our karma.

I went downstairs and brewed coffee. Amanda and Candice were already at the dining room table, all made up and dressed, with phones in their hands. They eagerly accepted my offer of scrambled eggs. Glenn lurched into the room and plopped in a chair. He didn't want eggs and peeled a banana. Mandy was already in AP Chemistry and impatient to finish high school. Candi was anxious about the pending chemistry final and Amanda offered to help. To my surprise, Candice welcomed the support. She explained that Amanda was better with Chem than I was. Glenn settled for a peanut butter and jelly sandwich while the eggs were served. I wanted to wait for Adrienne, so delayed my own breakfast. After a kiss from the girls and a high-five from Glenn, they waved goodbye and left for school. Amanda whispered in my ear. "Have a good Anniversary breakfast." How'd that girl get so intuitive?

By the time Adrienne got to the dining room, the kitchen was cleaned up and a load of laundry was drying in the basement. "The coffee smells good," she mumbled with a scowl. With that positive remark, my hope surged. I moved in to kiss her. She turned her head aside and offered me her cheek.

"Listen, honey," I said. "Take your time. It's your day off. When you're ready, let's go out. Maybe a stroll or some casual shopping. OK?"

After taking a sip of coffee, she glanced at me with a look of confusion, or disdain, or dislike. "Whatever," she replied.

I like the verdant yards and the busy creatures of suburban wildlife; but I'm a city boy at heart. Several favorite cafes and various haunts keep me energized. The crowds, the chatter, the eccentric characters, the ethnic diversity, and the unplanned moments of comedy and pathos provide an ever-changing diversion. Going into the city with no plan at all is often the better option. I'm a flaneur, a casual urban wanderer. It all just happens. But Adrienne needs certainty, structure, and purpose. C'mon, Barrett, follow the Buddha. Acceptance, Compassion. Surrender your ego.

I flourish in the urban atmosphere and wander through the hectic streets like a child in a playroom. Adrienne complained of the smell of the city. She was agitated by "all the dirt", but I found the streets fairly clean. Any crowded urban center gets a little messy, but for Adrienne, it bordered on intolerable.

The hostess recognized me as we entered the Rain or Shine bistro in the Chelsea area. We exchanged a few pleasantries and she granted us a corner table near a window. I watched the human parade outside while Adrienne scanned the menu. Being familiar with the place, I ordered quickly, but Adrienne interrogated the waiter about every ingredient in each item. I appreciate her concern about organic health, but the questions were interminable. The waiter struggled to maintain his poise, even when Adrienne, after a total analysis of every ingredient, shifted her focus to a different item on the menu and resumed the inquiry. When the orders were finally made, the waiter rushed off and I excused myself to "go to the bathroom". I approached the waiter and apologized to him for the ritual. I also praised his endurance. He smiled and thanked me. I enjoyed the brunch; I think Adrienne did. She gave a nod and a grunt.

Adrienne needed supplies for the salon and the well-known Maquillage Boutique was nearby. When we walked out of the boutique, music was emanating from the local park. A jazz quartet was doing a fine job near the water fountain. Nearby, acrobats were rehearsing their routines with impressive balance and dramatic flips. At the other side of the park, the acoustic twang of folk music radiated over people lounging on grass or playing chess or backgammon. I was in my element, letting the day swarm around me. But Adrienne was restless and kept checking the items in her shopping bag.

"Let's head home," she requested in a way that sounded like an order. "I'm getting tired."

"Tired?" I asked with some annoyance as my Buddhist nature was slipping. "You slept late. It was an easy drive. It's early afternoon."

"What?" she challenged me. "I have to feel guilty for being tired?"

I slipped into a defensive stance. "I just thought we could enjoy a day in town. Maybe a movie."

"Why would I want to go to a movie in the middle of the day?" she asked like an accusation.

"I just thought, since you're feeling tired…"

"I wanna go home," she stated with finality.

We drove back home in near silence. I watched the city, on a comfortable end-of-summer day, recede as we headed back to our suburban sprawl. The inner Buddhist encouraged me to accept it all with love; but my more imperfect self wanted to shout and curse. I'll never be a bodhisattva, in this life or any other! I felt a thick tension building in my gut and rising up to my throat. Something was clutching at my heart. It felt like a hungry child.

I opened the window but Adrienne said the traffic was too noisy. I turned on some jazz on the radio. Adrienne asked me to lower the volume. She wasn't satisfied until it was close to inaudible.

Keep breathing. In and out. Anger serves no purpose. Any anger is bad karma. I became a student of the anger, how it's related to angry thoughts, how it's just a form of energy, how it can be reduced with breathing and reframing.

We got home before rush hour but the school day was already done. The TV was on in the den and someone was upstairs. Quiet enough to not alert the kids, I tried some intimate communication. "Are you ok?" I inquired. "Is something bothering you?"

"Oh, now you care?" she exclaimed. I was stunned. "You drag me into that dirty city on my day off and take me to some cheap diner…"

"It's a popular bistro," I interrupted. My inner Buddhist shrugged his shoulders, turned away, a headed back to his sangha.

"Bistro!" she snorted. "A fancy name for a cheap diner!"

"If you didn't want to go, why didn't you say so"

"Because I wanted to please you, to make you happy," she replied with more bitterness than coffee left on the heater too long.

"Well, I'm not pleased and I'm not happy!" I exclaimed. She glared at me with pursed lips. It was not the kind of day I had anticipated. I wanted to say something, but words failed me. I shook my head and waved her away. "I'm going upstairs."

As I climbed the stairs, she shouted to me. "Well, I'm not happy, either!" I stopped climbing and turned to her. Something, finally, had emerged. I waited eagerly for additional information. "Never mind," she muttered. "I need some private time." She scurried off to the kitchen. I thought about following her, but, anticipating further rejections and escalation, I deferred.

After a quick pasta dinner, the evening proceeded as usual. Mandy went to spend the night with her boyfriend. They were planning to apply to the same colleges. In reviewing Candi's homework, I was impressed with her knowledge of Avogadro's Number and mole ratios. Amanda is a good tutor. Candice gave me a hug and then went to her room for some confidential conversations. I thought about Candice blooming into adolescence and considered the young girls who weren't as fortunate.

I noticed Glenn was isolated in his room. His door was open and he was slumped in bed, staring into space. I knocked on the door. "Hey, buddy! What's up?"

"Nothing," he answered.

"Yeah," I replied. "Nothing can be trouble." I took a chair near his desk.

"You and Mom argue a lot," he stated.

I nodded. "People argue. No biggie."

"It's because she changed jobs," he reasoned. "She was a nurse."

"How do you figure…"

"She used to help sick people. She did important work. Now she cuts hair and clips nails."

I wasn't sure where he was going. I tried to put some clarity on it. "Look, Glenn. Nursing hours are tough. She had to cover on weekends sometimes, and evenings. She liked the work but…"

"She changed jobs ten years ago," he added. I nodded. For a while, we sat in silence. "Was it because of me?"

I was dismayed. "What? No! It's not like that." His logic put him to blame for our marital turmoil.

"When I was born, she had to quit nursing," he said with flat affect.

"It's not you," I tried to assure him. "People make decisions in life. We decided to have another child. Mom was already complaining about her work hours. She wanted to be home more. Amanda and Candice needed her more. So did I. It's just the way it is. People make changes when their lives change. They adapt."

Glenn sat up on the bed and peered down at the wooden floor. "So if this is what she wanted, if you wanted to be together more, why are you guys so miserable?"

I was impressed with my sensitive son. But I was also troubled for him. He was burdening himself with things not of his making. "Hey, people go through hard times. Sometimes we argue with the people we're closest to."

He looked me straight in the eyes. "Dad, are you happy?" His gaze was like an x-ray machine.

I stammered. "Sure," I lied. "Don't you ever get annoyed with a friend? It passes, right?"

He was pondering beyond my answer. "You guys have an anniversary coming soon."

"Yeah?"

"Is that part of the problem? Twenty years."

"What do you mean?"

He answered with a troubling metaphor. "Do relationships have an expiration date?"

He was not being sarcastic. Perhaps he picked up some anthropology from Amanda. Apparently, he was studying Adrienne and me like a scientist and developing his own hypothesis about human relations. Something inside me broke. I could feel it. A decision had been reached in my core that was not yet born in my consciousness. The robot was stirring.

****

I must've dozed off. The book was in my lap and I jerked my head upright. Her apartment was dark. No messages. A chill of intuition rushed through me. Maybe the preferences of her political client take extra time. But I would usually get some sign from her. I rang her phone but it went directly to her voicemail with no ring.

The cops had already circled the block a few times so I couldn't leave the car by the hydrant. Fortunately, after 10pm even the most astringent parking regulations surrender to the night city. I found a spot near the corner and walked to her stoop. One more time, the cops drove by and gave me an apprehensive leer. They drove by since I didn't fit their usual profile.

****

With cautious stealth, Barrett slowly opened the bedroom door and walked into Sabrina's boudoir. He remembered several of his own erotic adventures in that chamber. Once their passions were depleted, they usually collapsed into the sleep of satisfaction. But, upon awakening, they would look around the room and snicker. Pillows and clothes and blankets were tossed around the room in random chaos. After a shower, which they often shared, it took a while to recover various garments from the ruins. But when he entered the bedroom this time, he experienced a sense of dread. The room was perfectly composed. The bed was neatly made. All clothes were in drawers and closets. "Who were the exotic clients?" he wondered. And where the hell was Sabrina? It was orderly to the point of being annoying. Nothing was out of place.

Barrett sat on Sabrina's sofa; the weird red one with no legs and elaborate geometric designs. He leaned against one of the large pillows that were propped against the wall. He fiddled with the tassels while pondering the situation. Did Sabrina cancel the event for some reason? Did she have another customer? Was there a sudden change in locale for the rendezvous? Did he confuse her messages? None of these prospects assured him. Sabrina would've left a text message.

As he scanned the premises, he studied the tasseled side table. Its base was like a beaded parabola. The tabletop was supported on a sphere with floral engravings. The piece of furniture was an apt metaphor for Sabrina; exotic, enticing, mysterious.

Something was on the porcelain top. He slipped over to the corner piece and picked up the shiny object. It was a very elaborate ring. The center stone was first to grab his attention. It was deep blue, maybe a sapphire, with a ghost white symbol engraved into it. It looked like an eagle. But the bird had two heads facing in opposite directions; something like Janus but with separate necks. Its wings were spread to both sides, as were its legs that terminated in open sharp talons. It had one feathered tail between the legs. Then he noticed the diamonds that covered the shoulders and ran down most of the shank. With these smaller accent stones alone he could have retired comfortably. There was an inner hallmark engraving he couldn't decipher. The letters were of foreign origin.

Barrett carried the ring to the dining room and sat at the table. Who would leave such a valuable object? Why is the apartment so neat and clean? Where is Sabrina? He knew a couple of honest appraisers. Maybe they'd be able to supply a few clues.

7

College Life and Internet Porn

A college dorm is never pretty. People are forgiven if they assume that girls keep their premises neat. You might also think the girls would have an influence on the boys in a co-ed dorm; but it seemed to have gone the other way. Amanda and her three roommates were just as messy as their male counterparts. Two bunk beds in a cramped room, with a narrow closet and two meager cabinets, would have tested the nerves of most suburban females. But Amanda was blessed with three playful and idealistic roommates. Complain about the cafeteria? Hey, people were hungry in Africa. Get annoyed with the claustrophobic quarters? Did you forget about our growing homeless problem? Besides, someday you'll look back on these trivial annoyances with wistful nostalgia.

Roommates certainly weren't chosen by area of interest. Amanda plunged into Chemistry while Irene analyzed the dynamics of neoliberal Economics for her Business major. Cynthia vacillated between English Literature and Philosophy. She also vacillated in her sexual orientation, which made Amanda both nervous and curious at the same time. Charlene, deeply involved in identity politics, was engaged in African-American History with a backup in Pre-Law. One month, she dazzled her friends with smooth straight hair extensions; then switched to a proud all-out Afro. When the college promised a diverse educational experience, they were serious.

The bathrooms were in the hall and commonly shared. Amanda made a few male friends when she left the shower, her hair still dripping, and wrapped only in a large towel. After the initial shock, the shared facilities normalized the experience. The girls and the guys were human beings to each other, not objectified unattainable "others". There were several sinks in each bathroom. Often a guy would be shaving by one sink while Amanda brushed her teeth in another. It was sort of like being married. Once you share a bathroom together, there is a bond.

One thing Amanda wanted was a part-time job. She felt guilty about college costs and didn't want to keep calling her parents for any expense. As a waitress or a receptionist, she could take care of incidentals; and she wouldn't have to explain or justify every procurement. A six-pack of beer or a concert ticket could be a private matter. If she needed to take a cab home from a lounge once in a while, there was no need to cause her parents any worry.

She was just finishing her calculations on gas properties when Gilbert knocked on the open door. "Hey! Busy?"

Without turning from her notes, she replied, "Another five minutes. Have a seat." He looked around. "Sit on the bed." He waited while Amanda put the finishing touches on the assignment. She closed the book and finally engaged him. "What's up?"

"So, it's Friday and…"

"You computer nerds always start sentences with 'so'. What's that about?"

He thought about that for a moment. "So…oh no!" They both laughed. "Any way, wanna go out? We're going to The Lasagna Lounge."

"Hmm. Good pasta and fun dancing. I could use that. But my cash is low 'til next month."

"No sweat," exclaimed Gilbert as if he were waiting for such a situation. "My treat."

"So it's a date?" asked Amanda with a squint. "What are you after?"

60

"Your companionship," answered Gil. "I already got your body."

"Did you? I forgot."

"Bitch!"

Amanda giggled. "That's no way to talk to your date," she teased.

"So you'll come?"

"Yeah, but…"

"Uh oh. The infamous 'but'. What's the matter?"

"Well, I promised my roommates I'd go out with them tonight. They were also gonna pay for me."

Gilbert rubbed his chin dramatically. "Let's see. Would it be OK for me to go with four hot chicks? I guess so."

"You're a pig!" Amanda slapped his arm.

Gil looked at Amanda with a sudden serious expression. "No I'm not." He stroked her cheek.

"No. You're a good guy." She leaned in and kissed him the way young lovers who share a co-ed dorm kiss. She rested her head on his shoulder. "I'll call them. Maybe they'll meet us there."

"Too bad. I was hoping to make a grand entrance…"

"Don't blow it, Gilbert." She spoke his name with precise articulation.

"You know I hate that. Please, just call me Gil."

"If you're good. But when you get obnoxious…"

"OK, I get it."

****

Lasagna Lounge, just outside the campus boundary, was a favorite watering hole for the college crowd. With great Italian food and after-dinner music, it was the perfect venue for a Friday blowout. Since the cops always kept it under surveillance for under-age drinkers, alcohol and pot were consumed in the parking lot. Needless to say, there were frequent trips to the cars to retrieve "forgotten" wallets or credit cards, or any other object. So long as Lasagna Lounge obeyed the laws, the police had no interest in minor drug offenses near a private college.

Amanda particularly liked to draw a deep inhale and then blow it into Gil's mouth. He returned the favor. Small sample bottles of canned heat embellished the experience while music rumbled from the car radio. They laughed when Cynthia walked by, holding the hand of a sweet co-ed. "So it's girls tonight," Amanda quipped.

"Give her an hour," stated Gil. "She might change her mind." The ganja was having its effect. That seemed like the funniest joke ever. They fell onto each other and cackled. "I think we're having an earthquake." It didn't make sense, but the laughter continued.

Once the giddies wore off, the hungries took over. They left the car and retuned to their table, where Charlene was engrossed in conversation with one of the musicians and Irene was strolling the bar. She was too young to order a drink but old enough to beat the system. One guy who may have been a professor took notice and offered to buy her a drink. She accepted. "It's cool," thought Amanda. "So easy to connect when you're in college. High school was awful."

The salad was conveniently chopped and the dressing soaked through just enough. The pasta was perfectly al dente. The sauce was thick and spicy. Gil dipped his garlic bread eagerly and Amanda slapped his hand when he grabbed for the last slice. So he broke it in half and they plunged into the sauce together. Even if their senses weren't attenuated, it would've been a gastronomic orgy.

Cynthia returned from the parking lot with her new friend, who was introverted enough to border on paranoid. Charlene came to the table to tell them all about the saxophone player who was about to perform. Irene chose to stay at the bar with her professor. Gil leaned to Amanda. "Irene's gonna get an 'A' this semester."

Amanda pursed her lips. "Be nice, Gilbert." He sulked and she relented. "Thanks for this date. I hate depending on you for the money."

"Maybe I can help," he interjected. "I heard about this web site. They post jobs for college students."

"Later," quipped Amanda who was feeling edgy and restless. "Dance with me." The band was performing the obligatory list of standards. Every one from every age could identify with some of the tunes. With the common bond of nostalgia to blanket them all, the patrons were happy, sharing an evening of easy motion and casual familiarity. The band offered an open mike. Amanda joined the band for a rendition of "These Boots are Made For Walking." The feminists shouted out, "You go, girl!" while the sexists yelled, "Walk them boots over here, baby!" Not to be outdone, Charlene hopped on the stage for her version of "Saving All My Love For You", a wistful tune in which a mistress longs for her married lover. Dogmatic morality succumbs to endearing empathy. That put everyone in the mood for the slow tunes that followed. Cynthia flowed across the dance floor with her sweet young ingénue. Charlene stood near the stage to let each note from her saxophone player vibrate into her.

Irene joined the entourage when they returned to their booth. She slid next to Amanda and quickly ordered a cocktail with a phony ID that was flawlessly authentic. She'd overheard the conversation about part-time work. "You kidding?" she interjected with confidence. "You don't need some proletarian web site; not with your looks." Amanda turned to Irene and blinked in surprise. "Put down your science books for a minute and take a look in the mirror."

Gil never liked Irene very much. She was too pragmatic, too callous, in a capitalistic kind of way. He wanted to use computer technology to improve peoples' lives, cure genetic diseases, improve food supplies; Irene would use computers to enhance efficiency and lay off a thousand workers. They'd both get an "A" in their term papers; but Irene's projects would leave a lot of "collateral damage". It was hard to debate her impeccable logic without being a "bleeding heart liberal". But she was correct about Amanda. The girl was gorgeous!

Irene continued. "When you're not blowing everyone's mind with quantum insanity, you have that minor in Anthropology, right?" Amanda nodded obediently. "Well, in your studies on the human animal, what's the story about Beauty? Your figure is right on target. Your face is perfectly symmetrical." Irene looked at Amanda with dramatic envy. "Even that sweet little nose."

The rational scientist started to rebel. "So I'm attractive. What are you saying?"

Without missing a beat, Irene made her presentation. "The college years are a perfect time to get into modeling. You can't lose. You'll be pampered with makeup artists and fashion designers and photographers. All you'd have to do is sit still and be pretty. You'll make enough money to leave college debt-free and you won't have to drain your parents dry."

"I can see you now," said Gil to Amanda, attempting a comic escape. "Strutting down that runway with the band playing; celebrities in the audience worshipping you. It's a girl's dream." Amanda jabbed an elbow in his side. She laughed, but with more effort than earlier. The pot was wearing off. "Of course, some dreams are nightmares," he said to wrap up the discussion.

"You don't have to believe me," Irene countered. "Here. I know a guy." She tore a napkin and wrote on it; then handed it to Amanda. "You're lucky to have a friend in Business. You want a Big Bang? Call him."

Amanda stared at the napkin, folded it and stuck it in her purse. "Ok, thanks, Irene," she said awkwardly. "But no more business. It's Friday night and we're dancing."

Irene smiled and winked at her. "Business never sleeps." She ordered another drink. Besides, she gets a ten percent finder's fee.

****

Glenn was flushed and stammering. Although he wasn't exactly surprised, Barrett also found the moment to be awkward. He knew Glenn liked to play videogames, but this sudden burst of puberty was both humorous and startling.

"I have to admit, you found a very creative site." Barrett tried to make light of it. It wasn't working.

"I...I'm sorry, Dad." Glenn was fidgeting like a trapped rat that had no escape and awaited his fate. "I just...I was wondering...I needed...". He went silent, realizing he was only digging a deeper hole for himself.

"Hey, c'mon. Relax, Glenn." Barrett laughed and tried to reassure his son with a smile. "You're a guy. You're curious. Basic porn. It's readily available." The couple on the screen was attractive and passionate. As far as he could tell, the sex was consensual. "You didn't commit any crime." He exited the site. The apparent lovers vanished and his familiar desktop reappeared, a majestic view of a forest scene. "I don't get it. Why use my computer?"

"You have to be over 18," was Glenn's weak explanation.

Barrett laughed gently. "So when they asked, 'Are you over 18?', you were afraid to say 'yes' on your own computer? You thought you'd be caught in some criminal offense?" Glenn bowed his head, embarrassed. "If they can track your computer, why would they bother to ask you?" He noted. "They're just covering their own ass. If they ever get caught corrupting youth, or whatever, they could say you lied to them." Barrett dropped the legal issue and shifted toward Glenn. "It's ok, man." Then, trying to lighten the mood, he asked, "Did you find out what you needed to know?"

Somewhat relieved, and eager to share a masculine bond, Glenn smirked. "I guess so. Sort of."

"You know, the porn is often different from the real thing." Glenn's eyes shot wide open. He clearly wanted more information. Barrett was committed. "What I mean is, well, the sequence is often wrong."

"Like how?"

Might as well just lay it out for him. "Well, really! Go into oral sex right after orgasm?"

"Oh." Glenn flushed like a ripened beet.

"And finishing with hand jobs and come on the girl's face? What the hell?"

"Uh huh."

"And going to it for, what, forty minutes? One orgasm after the other? The woman maybe could do that, but the guy? And she would get sore after a while." Glenn's eyes roamed rapidly, not knowing where to focus. "Too much information?"

"I'm not sure, Dad." To his relief, Barrett stopped giving him more data. "I don't think a girl would ever want to do it with me anyway."

Barrett tried to recall being twelve years old: The junior high school madness, the painful awkwardness, and the changing bodies. He remembered intolerant teachers and the bullies who were converted into hallway monitors. He thought of some of the girls and how they terrified him. He remembered several precocious co-eds and how badly he wanted to ask them a hundred questions. "Listen, Glenn, growing up can be scary. Just remember, the girls are just as scared as you are. Never forget that they're also people; they have hopes and dreams. They're also blundering and feeling foolish."

Dropping adolescent barriers, Glenn took the risk to share. "In the movies, they're so happy to do it with the guy. Is that true? Do they want to do it so much? Do they get horny?"

Barrett replied with plain natural openness. "They have the same desires as you. But they have to get to know you. There has to be trust and safety."

"Is the girl gonna expect me to know everything?"

Barrett chuckled. "If you know too much, the girl's gonna wonder how you found out. If you're both virgins, you can learn together."

"Should I tell her I'm a virgin?"

"No need to, just hint about it." Barrett caught himself. "But let's slow down a minute. If you like a girl, say hello, smile, talk to her. Share your interests. Make jokes; laugh together…but not too much. Listen to her, what's important to her. Get to know each other. Life isn't just a porno movie. OK?"

Glenn nodded. "Yeah. Thanks, Dad. I liked this."

"Me too. You can always talk to me."

8

The Pawn Shop And the Mogul

S herman heard the jangle of bells as he opened the door to the
pawnshop. He always trusted Abe when he needed to price
something. Once, when he gave up the dream of a successful music
career, he hocked a drum set and got a generous price for it. He
remembered how Abe offered to extend the loan period. The old guy
never liked to profit from broken dreams; but Barrett reassured him.
"You're helping me to afford the next stage of my life." With a
shrug, Abe accepted the pawn and made a pretty decent profit on
the resale. So every one was satisfied. Now, as an insurance agent,
Barrett sometimes needed an honest number and relied upon Abe.

"Well, how are you, Barry?" Abe crowed. He put down the
necklace he was examining and returned it to a glass case under his
desk. "Long time no see." He brushed back his gray hair, which
never stayed in place, adjusted his eyeglasses, and extended his hand.

With a sincere smile, Barrett shook the old man's hand. "You
look good, Abe," he noted.

"Yeah, a regular Clark Gable," was Abe's retort. "And how's
your family? Three kids, right? The oldest one probably in college
now."

"Yep, you got it," replied Barrett. They never talked much about Abe's family since his wife was deceased and the kids hardly ever visit.

"It's quiet right now, lucky for you." Abe said as he noticed Barrett's left hand in his pocket. "You have a gift for me today?"

Barrett had a story prepared. "A client wants an honest appraisal for a family heirloom. A ring."

Abe crinkled his brow. "I'm basically a pawnbroker, Barry. Why would you come to me for this?"

"All right," Barrett confessed. "You got me. I need your honest estimate first. Then I'll know if an appraiser is on the level."

Abe was not totally satisfied with the explanation and paused to study Barrett's face and contemplate the situation. "OK," he concluded, "Let me see the ring."

Barrett pulled the ring out of his pocket and handed it to Abe. The old man pushed his glasses up his nose, gasped and stared at the object. "Oh my god! An Oksoko, carefully engraved on a beautiful sapphire." He turned the ring to its side. "These diamonds!" Abe gave the ring back to Barrett and scurried to his door. He locked the door and pulled down the shade. Anxiously, he looked around and approached Barrett. "Where the hell did you get that ring?"

"Like I said, a client..."

Abe interrupted him. "Don't give me that!" he snapped at him. "That thing is priceless! Should be in a museum!"

Barrett was shocked. "You kiddin' me? Priceless? It's not even in a case. What did you call it?"

"An Oksoko. It's a Turkish symbol. Selijuk Turk actually."

"Did you say, 'Selijuk'?" Barrett felt a chill run through his spine and a sharp jolt in the pit of his stomach.

Over the rim of his glasses, Abe looked at Barrett. "You've heard the term?" he inquired.

Barrett made a quick reply. "Yeah. There was a museum exhibit."

"Indeed," Abe confirmed. "It was an impressive empire for a time. Interesting art work." He peered into Barrett's face. "This client of yours? By any chance, was the ring acquired in less than legal ways?" Pawnshops were often used to fence stolen goods.

"I really don't know. Why do you ask?"

"Listen to me." The old man walked to a corner table and took a seat. He gestured for Barrett to join. Like two pirates in a dark tavern, they spoke in hushed tones. "Sapphires and rubies are made of corundum. Sapphires are very hard, almost as hard as diamonds. So, to etch such a fine symbol on the stone requires great skill. Besides, this sapphire itself is priceless. Vivid saturation, perfect tone. And those diamonds! Let me see the ring again."

Barrett placed the ring in Abe's trembling hand. Abe pulled a magnifier from a drawer. He moved the ring in several positions and studied it carefully. "My god! The cut! I'd call it signature grade. The color is certainly better than F grade. You know? Brilliant. No yellow, my friend! And the clarity! Just about flawless! No inclusions that I can see. Like I said, I'm not a professional jeweler. But I had to learn a lot in this profession. Even the shapes, round and oval and marquise, they are wonderful."

Barrett whispered back to Abe. "So if I insured this piece, what value should I…"

"No way!" Abe interjected. "It's priceless. You must not try to sell it."

"I'm not selling it," Barrett countered with feigned annoyance. "I'm trying to value it for insurance coverage."

Abe sighed and them groaned. "Fort Knox couldn't cover the cost. Do you understand me?" He got up and walked to his counter and opened a small drawer. He pulled out a small velvet case. "Here. Use this case. How could you walk around with the thing in your pocket?"

"It's the way it was…given to me," Barrett stammered. "I figured it was a simple family heirloom."

Abe shook his head and peeked through the shade on the door. "You might be followed," he warned.

Barrett released a nervous laugh. "C'mon, Abe. Now you're being dramatic."

"You're holding a piece that surpasses the treasury of most nations! No, I am not being dramatic. And YOU be careful!" He looked out the door again. "Now go. And be careful. And don't trust other appraisers. Not with that thing."

Barrett left the pawnshop with the velvet case in a zipped inner pocket of his jacket. He was about to walk back to his office, but changed his mind and took a taxi.

****

After dinner and a few TV shows, I kissed Amanda, waved to the kids, and headed out for my "night work". I was determined to return to Sabrina's apartment in search of some meanings. I never before had a safe deposit box but now I did. Before locking it up, I checked the inscription on the inside of the ring. The letters were strange to me but I copied them in my notebook. I paid the initial fee with my personal credit card and left the bank with a sense of relief. Carrying around that bauble, after the visit to Abe, felt like I was waving around the winning lottery ticket in a ghetto. Here I am! Come and get me! With the ring hidden away in a secure bank I tossed off the paranoia like a used coffee cup.

Was I being watched? Why was such a precious item left casually on a corner table? Why was that the ONLY item in the apartment? Why did Brin disappear so abruptly without a word? I tried to connect the dots: a beautiful mysterious woman in the "oldest profession" as an independent; her proud identification with her Selijuk history; the ring carries a Selijuk inscription; a priceless ring with a perfect sapphire and flawless diamonds; her sudden disappearance the same night as Meet-The-Teacher. The apartment was so clean it was like no one had lived there. Erased, deleted. The ring left around carelessly in the barren apartment.

The keys still worked. I slipped quietly up the stairs and unlocked her apartment door once again. It was still eerily quiet in contrast to the outdoor sounds of the city. I switched on the ceiling light and did a quick scan. My intuition was screaming at me to pay close attention. It was like those challenges in some children's workbooks: How are these two pictures different? They seem to be the same at first; and then you spot the changes. An arm was shifted, the number of flowerpots had changed, the person's sleeves were shorter. I began to notice the changes in the room. The couch was moved away from the wall and two of the large pillows had fallen to the floor. One of the dining room chairs was further from the table. There was a glass left in the kitchen sink. I stepped into the bedroom. A pillow had been tossed. The corner table was closer to the center of the room.

Someone had been here. He or she or they had been searching. Now I was frightened. If they were searching for that invaluable ring, they could be watching the place. Perhaps I had seen too many mystery movies but I began to search for bugs. If there were any, one would have to be near the entrance door. It would have to be high enough to scan the entire room.

There it was! At the corner of the ceiling was a small wire with an electronic device aimed toward the door.

I broke into a sweat but also felt chilly. I quickly flipped off the light and left the apartment. Instead of going downstairs, I went up to the roof. It was a crisp evening. The cool air and my anxious sweat comingled and I started to shiver. The space between buildings was small enough so I jumped across to the next one. From that roof, I peered over the ledge. I didn't see anything or any one suspicious so I went to descend; but that roof door was either locked or jammed. Not wanting to disturb sleeping tenants, I decided to take one more leap of faith. The door to the third building was unlocked. I tiptoed down those stairs and nonchalantly exited the building. It was then that I saw three people at the entrance of Sabina's building. They were looking up toward her apartment. Controlling my impulses, I walked slowly and took deep breaths. Slipping around the next corner, I was on a main avenue and blended in with the evening crowd.

****

Henry Anderson looked like a rather ordinary name with just a hint of WASP. He learned the secrets of material success from his father and grandfather. Land. There is just so much under our feet to parcel out. As the population continues to grow, the demand for some of the remaining terrain increases exponentially. Wars are fought for an extra piece of earth. From the ashes of a war-torn Europe, his family packed up, brought their modest fortune, and planted roots in the real estate business of America.

At first, they were simple landlords who learned how to manipulate a lease or roll over equity into another investment. As neighborhoods gentrified, they learned how cities evolved. The poor find attractive locales; the rich follow their lead, and then evict the original inhabitants. Puritans and Pioneers evict Indians. Imperialists evict brown and yellow natives. The persecuted escape to another land and evict the indigent populations. The Andersons justified their strategies by calling it the way of the world, the inevitable dynamic of history. "Social Darwinism" was an insult to the name of a noble scientist. "Survival of the Fittest" rendered the victims unfit and deserving of their lot in life. The masses are pushed to the margins. But the margins expand as the power of development is like a hungry beast, forever devouring more and more acreage.

The process continues in a burgeoning spiral. Wealth opens doors. Ethics are flexible when you have good lawyers, skilled lobbyists, and politicians desperate for campaign financing. Real estate laws take you through the looking glass. There's profit in the abandonment of properties. Risks are taken with disastrous results; but become lucrative tax write-offs that may even cover future income. Losses are a tax break while profits are steered into "like-kind exchanges" and other carve-outs. The refugees from war-ravaged Europe evolved into the rulers of an empire in sixty years. The realtor can claim losses due to "depreciation" while his properties are increasing in value. It's the American Dream in nightmare proportions.

With the creation of limited liability companies, LLCs, the invasion into traditional neighborhood communities continues with minimal risk to the invader, who also benefits from the flow-through of "carried interest". As Leona Helmsley once said, "Only the little people pay taxes." The little people are the ones who try to follow the rules they were taught in school and church. The Andersons and the Helmsleys of the world make their own rules; they have the legal and political clout to do so. The little people are not allowed to benefit from the process; only "active" realtors, not the passive tenants or mortgagors.

The process of gentrification ravages the very communities that attracted investors in the first place. High-rise superstructures replace modest apartments with affordable rents. City parks are overshadowed by the incessant increase in luxury towers. The indigent population, which is most of us, can't afford the rents these structures demand. Our salaries haven't really compensated for the increased cost of living for the past fifty years.

So who buys these condominiums, suites, and penthouses? Where is their money coming from? How much of that money is legitimate by floundering global standards?

Henry Anderson, President and CEO of Anderson Development Corporation, and its extensive network of subordinate LLCs, with their offshore accounts throughout the Caribbean, rotated his chair and peered out from his penthouse office. A healthy man in his mid-fifties, he often assumed that pose when he had to resolve a business obstruction. He didn't care about the financial loss itself. His tax attorneys would handle that irritation. But the network had links. He had to keep the smoke and mirrors in place. Layers of dummy companies and pseudo-charities would keep investigators busy for decades while cash flows could be laundered and flipped.

Just the same, a sufficient degree of paranoia was necessary. Any small piece in the puzzle could lead to a bigger piece until the dots could be connected. Any courtroom trial, with extensive media coverage, would be bad for business. It wasn't a conviction or settlement that was important. That could be handled. It was the loss of trust in his network's credibility that would frighten away collaborators who required secrecy and concealment. From public exposure, word-of-mouth spreads quickly. Even his mistress, almost half his age, expressed concern. For a beauty queen who usually kept out of his business, the information even trickled down to her. That was bad. He had to plug the leak quickly. He couldn't do it directly.

Middlemen would make the contacts and clear the leaks by any means necessary.

9

Gizem

I t was good timing since Kenny was out to lunch. The young girl emerged from the elevator with her bicycle and proceeded to the office of Huntington Insurance. She struggled to get her bike through the door until Tanya got up with a huff and helped her. Tanya glared at her fellow minions with disdain. "Too busy to show some compassion?" The girl thanked her and they exchanged a few words. Tanya turned and directed her toward Barrett's cubicle. He wore ear buds and was talking into his cell while staring intently at his computer screen, oblivious to Tanya or the girl. Tanya took the bicycle, which the girl was uncomfortable surrendering, and placed it near the common wall. "Don't worry, child. I'll keep an eye on it for you." Somewhat reassured, the girl walked down the corridor.

Barrett was sharing policy rates and conditions with a client. The light from the computer screen caused his face to glow. "Yes, I understand. A reassessment may alter your coverage. But, with a clean record, only a small incident like that, the policy would only show a nominal bump." Such bullshit, he thought to himself. With all this experience, I should get into politics. It took a while to notice the wide-eyed girl at his cubicle.

Her large dark eyes had a yellow tint. Her long silken dark hair reminded him of Sabrina. She seemed to be about nine years old, slender, but tall for her age. She had the same bronze complexion with silver undertones. She waited patiently, like a lobby statue that's easily overlooked, without fidgeting or shifting her weight. "Don't worry," he spoke into the phone, eager to finish the conversation. "As soon as we get the update, I'll share all the options with you. Of course. I will. Thanks. Be well." He clicked off his phone and gave the child his undivided attention. "Hello. May I help you?"

"Are you Mister Barrett Sherman?" she asked with a direct stare that chilled him. The girl seemed too poised for her age.

"Yes," he replied. "I am."

"Please excuse me, but I need to see some I.D." There was no quiver in her voice, no anxiety in her stance. This girl was accustomed to addressing adult men. She did it with uncanny authority.

"Of course," he said, fascinated by the child. "Will a driver's license do?" He could hear Chuck smirking in the other cubicle while Harry told him to shut up. Harry, the philosopher, was also intrigued by the precocious youngster. Sylvia made a comment about boys never growing up.

The girl studied the license, flipped it over several times, as if she could identify a forgery. Barrett had no doubt she could. "OK," she finally replied. "I have something for you." With graceful motion, she opened her satchel, removed an envelope and relinquished it to Barrett. "I'm required to have your signature." She handed him a form. The letterhead came at him like a punch in the face.

"Oksoko," he murmured but the girl heard him.

"Indeed," said the girl as if to validate his comment. "Now, will you please sign?"

Barrett stared at the two-headed eagle with flailing talons. Every obsession he had struggled to suppress came surging into his consciousness. He did his best to contain the trembling in his hand as he signed the acknowledgement of receipt. "Do you know…"

"You must remember my name," she interrupted. "But never write it down. Anywhere."

Barrett wanted to scold the girl. He had few patriarchal tendencies, but the impudence of this young girl was provocative. But he contained the impulse. "Ok," he acquiesced. "Your name."

She looked around, sensitive to the listeners in other cubicles. She moved in until her legs were brushing his knee. With no concern about discretion, she whispered in his ear. "Gizem. Whisper it back to me." She turned her head to the side. Strands of her silken jet hair brushed his face.

"Gizem," he repeated. She looked into his eyes and nodded. "Now we must trust you." She withdrew from him and moved toward the corridor.

"Wait!" He was speaking below the reception of snooping co-workers. "Is every one OK?" His facial expression pleaded for more information.

Gizem smiled gently. "We must trust you," she repeated. "I must go now." She turned and vanished.

Barrett sat with the envelope in his hand. He could hear Gizem thanking Tanya for watching her bicycle. "No problem, sweetheart. Take care now." Once again, Tanya held the door while the child pulled her bike out of the office.

When Barrett came out of his trance, he saw Harry, Chuck, and Sylvia hovering over him. He needed a quick cover story. "A paranoid client, frustrated actor. He likes to add too much drama. I wonder what he paid the kid to behave like that." They were staring at the envelope. "Family information," he explained. "Children's names, dates of birth, medical issues. The usual."

Chuck responded with, "Man, it takes all kinds, eh?" Sylvia added, "Whatever." Harry held his ground silently until the other two returned to their own cubicles. When things settled back into the usual boredom, he asked, "So what's her name?"

Barrett replied with a laugh. "You know what she whispered to me?" Harry waited with palms upward. "Gotcha!" Harry displayed skepticism and Barrett insisted. "Really! Gotcha. She's probably a young actress showing off her skill. Pretty eccentric."

Harry chewed on that explanation for a while and then decided to spit it out. "Whenever you want to tell me the truth, let's have lunch." He patted Barrett on the shoulder and returned to his own station.

That night, as he headed out, Barrett turned to Tanya.

"Don't bother," she said. "It's not my business."

"Really," he tried. "I have no idea…"

"Good night, Barry."

"Good night, Tanya."

****

I kept fidgeting with my jacket, checking every minute to make sure the envelope was safely ensconced in my inner pocket. Trying to be cool while a chill throughout my skin caused me to shiver, I was so preoccupied that I had no idea how I got home. Perhaps the car knew the way by itself. Parked in my own driveway, I rubbed my eyes, which began to burn. Candi saw the lights from my car and peeked through the curtains, then slouched back onto the couch to continue her cell phone chat. Busted. If I stayed in the car, there would be questions. So, I patted my inner pocket one more time and trudged to the house.

Candi acknowledged my existence with a quick nod and a dull wave, then resumed her chat. Glenn was probably in the den with the latest videogame while Adrienne, from the kitchen, offered a detached greeting.

At least the family dog was excited to see me. He was a mellow old retriever. For some mysterious reason, we had named him Ernie. "Hey, boy, glad to see me?" I fondled Ernie's chin and he whimpered happily. "Wanna go out, boy?" Good old Ernie was about to pay me back for all the walks and visits to the vet. He would be my alibi. At the utterance of the word, "out", Ernie jumped for joy. I announced my intentions and Adrienne replied with a grunt. I retrieved a doggy bag, pulled the leash off the wall, made the hookup, and took a stroll.

Ernie pulled on the leash at first, eager to do his business, but settled down in ten minutes. There was a boulder under a streetlamp near the town park. "Let's enjoy the evening for a while, buddy." I patted Ernie and he sniffed a patch of ground. Once it met with the approval of his nose, he hunkered down.

In slow deliberate movements, in sharp contrast to my percussive heart, I pulled out the envelope and casually tore it open.

Barrett:

You must destroy this letter, and the envelope as soon as you read it. I am not being dramatic. It is of vital importance that you shred it or burn it. Do not leave it in pieces that can be re-assembled. It must be obliterated. If you happened to find a ring in my apartment, you must safeguard it carefully. Never display the ring! Keep it safe.

What did you think of the girl? Did she impress you? Intrigue you? Mystify you? That's what Gizem actually means, "Mystery". I gave her that name. She no longer remembers her birth name. She is only nine years old, but she is very worldly. There is a reason for that. The girl was one of many children abducted into a global sex trafficking network. That's how I met her. It was a brothel in The Ukraine. I was a free agent, an independent. Gizem was not. The poor girl was only seven when she arrived, trembling but stoic. I agreed to take her under my care. The madam was sympathetic and kind. I said I would teach her the business. There was no choice in that matter. I hated the disgusting men who would desire such an innocent child.

After about one year, we had our chance. I learned about an underground society with powerful dreams. They were opposed to all the strict religious fanatics who were destroying our civilization. They spoke of Mohammed and how he treated all his wives with respect; not like pawns in a male-dominated world. The members of this society wanted true freedom for the Asian world. From them I learned about my Selijuk heritage, and an empire that spread from the Aral Sea to the Mediterranean. In addition to modern Turkey, it included the Levant, Iran, and most of Arabia. Maybe even Somalia!

Being a free worker, I could leave the brothel whenever I wished. Using contacts from the society, we traveled across many countries, dodging the traffickers along the way, and finally settled in Germany. From the German Consulate, I was directed to an office of UN.GIFT or UNODC, which helps people escaping from the trafficking. I met many young girls, very much like Gizem.

When you think of Gizem, can you turn away and forget her? Can you let your heart go cold because it would be so painful otherwise? Perhaps you would be so kind to help us? I met many young girls, very much like Gizem.

Gizem will visit you again. But not at your place of work. A repeat contact there is too dangerous. I will contact you again soon. Do not respond to any correspondence unless I use this password: Khazaria. You must be very careful. We are resisting a two hundred billion dollar business. For that kind of wealth, any one would do anything. Khazaria.

Sincerely Yours,

Sabrina

I read the letter about five times, taking in more information with each analysis. My god! A secret society? Children abducted into human trafficking? The image of vulnerable seven-year-old Gizem being used sexually by some decrepit monster! *I met many young girls, very much like Gizem.* The thought was too horrifying to conjure.

I was descending into a world I had heard about in passing, on a brief news report. I wanted to protect Gizem, hold her, console her, let her know she could be a child again.

Clearly there was a difference between voluntary sex workers and victims of trafficking. With Sabrina, it was a free choice; perhaps under economic pressure but with no coercion. With victims, there is no consent, no options, and certainly no ability to say "No!"

I read one line over and over: *You must be very careful. We are resisting a two hundred billion dollar business. For that kind of wealth, any one would do anything.* I couldn't fathom that kind of money. It was like trying to visualize infinity.

The office shredder would be busy tomorrow.

10

The Precinct Meeting

N o one would describe her as meek or timid. If anything, the prostitute walked into the precinct with a proud posture and a challenging strut. She pulled out of the officer's grip as they approached the desk sergeant. "You've had enough grabs, altar boy," she advised the cop. "Any more feels and I charge you. And you can't afford me." Behind the cop, his female partner reacted with an obvious grimace. "What's your problem, Virgin Mary?" She tapped on the glass where the desk sergeant waited impatiently.

"You got any ID?" the sergeant asked.

"Of course," she answered. "I'm an upstanding citizen, chief."

"I'm not the Chief," the sergeant replied and quickly regretted.

Sabrina tapped on the glass with exquisite long nails. "Well, you should be. You got what it takes, man."

"Look," snapped the sergeant. "It's been a long day. Just show me your ID. Good girl."

"Now do me a favor," she snarled. "Send me to Detective Salvatore Mancini."

"You don't give the orders here," replied the sergeant with growing annoyance. "You gonna post bail?"

"We'll see. First, I want Mancini. I heard he's an honest cop. Hard to believe."

The sergeant returned her picture ID through the slot in the glass window. "Go sit down."

She stood her ground, arms crossed, glaring at the sergeant. "Mancini," she demanded.

"Sit down, princess. Now."

The two street cops flanked her. "Make it easy on yourself and cooperate. OK?"

"Whatever," said Sabrina with a shrug. "Just no more patting down, Romeo."

For the benefit of the room, the male cop announced, "I never patted you. She did." He pointed a thumb toward his partner. "So shut up!"

Sabrina shook her head. "No way to talk to a lady."

"No lady here," chirped the female in blue.

"Yeah," replied Sabrina as she shot the woman a stare. "No lady in here."

"Bitch!" hissed the female.

"Easy, sister," countered Sabrina. "We're all professionals, after all."

Sabrina took a seat, wrapped her arms across the chair, and let an ample amount of leg shake through the slit in her short skirt. The female stared at her. "Like what you see, sweetheart?" Sabrina taunted with a sneer.

The female grunted and trudged to the coffee machine in the vestibule. "I swear to god…" Incomprehensible cursing. "I gotta get outa Vice."

"Take it easy, Mother Teresa." The crowd in the vestibule was beginning to enjoy the entertainment and a few giggles were audible. "I promise I'll be good if you get me Mancini." The woman looked at her with a quizzical expression. "You see, I don't trust most cops. Some of them have been shit to me. But, girl, you pass my test. So, c'mon. Get me Mancini." Sabrina's copper beauty and pleading expression, breaking through hanging raven hair, got to them.

The male gave his partner a respite. "Look, I can understand that some cops may have knocked you around. So, just calm down and we'll do what we can. Deal?"

"Sure," she grumbled. "That's all I want."

****

"Hey, Sal, one of the hookers is giving us some trouble. She says she wants to see you." The cop was annoyed and in no mood for complications. Mancini crinkled his brow in confusion and grunted. "Why don't you just humor her?" the cop pleaded. "We don't need this hassle. We can't finish the damn report." Mancini yielded.

Detective Salvatore Mancini cleared away any confidential records from his desk and moved away objects that could be thrown like a weapon. After thirty years on the force, he learned to be cautious. He figured the woman got his name from the grapevine or a news report. But he was prepared for some kind of shakedown.

The cop reappeared with the rather exotic copper skinned beauty. "She's clean," declared the cop. "She's not carrying."

"Good to know," replied Mancini. He faced the woman. "You want to see me?"

She checked his nameplate on the desk but needed to be sure. "If you don't mind, may I see your personal I.D.?"

Mancini was taken back by that request. Nonetheless, the lady was within her rights. He reached into his jacket and pulled out his wallet. "Is this official business?" he asked. "Or just for the drama? Will my driver's license satisfy you?" She nodded and he passed the license to her. She shifted her gaze several times from the voucher to the detective. The cop got annoyed but Mancini raised his hand for patience.

While she studied his license, Mancini studied her. She had what they call "good hair", jet-black but thin and straight, falling to her exposed waist. Her short purple skirt was wrapped below her slender hips. Her deep dark eyes had a bit of an Asian slant, and she applied eye shadow with professional precision.

"OK," said the strange woman. "Thank you." She returned his license. "May I sit?" Mancini smiled and waved to the vacant chair. If her clinging skirt didn't supply enough of a preview, there was also a slit. However, when she crossed her legs, she did it with a style that was more regal than lewd. She was skillfully luring him in. "Who is this woman?" He wondered, but he maintained a neutral expression.

"OK," said Mancini. "Now it's my turn to ask some questions."

Sabrina remained poised and confident. "I need to speak with you privately," she replied. The cop cursed under his breath. He didn't like a cheap hooker making demands.

"You probably know that's against protocol," remarked Mancini.

"The policeman has my recorder," she remarked. She turned to the cop and offered him a childish pout. "If he would return it to me, we can record the meeting." She turned to Mancini. "You can keep it."

The cop protested but Mancini outranked him. "Wait outside my door," he directed. "I'm gonna play along for a while." After voicing his complaint, the cop left the office and closed the door. She handed Mancini the recorder. He checked the battery and it seemed legit. He clicked it on.

The woman crossed her hands, rested her elbows on his desk, and tapped her chin, while Mancini read the rap sheet. "OK, Sabrina, what do you want?"

Sabrina lowered her hands onto the desk. "I had to play the role for the benefit of the troops," she explained. "I know you're an honest cop."

"Most cops are honest family men," replied Mancini. "And women," he added to be politically correct.

She shrugged her shoulders. "If you say so." Her dark eyes peered into some dark region of his soul. "I need a favor from you. We can make a deal."

Mancini laughed. "Too soon, Sabrina. I'm supposed to interrogate you first."

She kept staring at him. "No need to. We're on the same side." The detective was slipping into paranoia, suspecting some form of blackmail. He double-checked the recorder. "I belong to a network. We know about a large shipment. They had to divert from the usual destination in Atlanta. The mayor there is in a tight election race, so he organized another cleanup."

"Go ahead. I'm listening."

"First, the favor." Mancini pursed his lips as Sabrina gained leverage. "Let me go. I'm not the problem; I'm part of the solution. And let five other girls go."

Mancini smirked. "You're bluffing. I should release six prostitutes with no charges on the basis of a story."

Sabrina glared at him. "Those girls are young and very frightened. I'm trying to…" She paused to compose herself. "I'm liberating them, getting them straight. They were only pawns for our use."

"Really?" Sabrina was amusing him, but he was growing weary of the ploy. "Pawns?"

"This bust at the strip club?" asked Sabrina. "Do you really think it was random?" Mancini was intrigued. "You received an anonymous tip."

"Yeah," replied Mancini, wondering how she knew that.

"It was so we could meet," she declared. "I needed cover. You got the call two days ago at eleven in the morning."

Mancini was frozen to his chair. He checked his daily log. She was right on target. "What the hell is this?" he asked. "If you know about a drug shipment…"

"I never said 'drugs'. There may be some drugs in the cargo, but that's secondary." She could tell Mancini was curious but still wary. "We don't have time to jerk around, Detective. I suggest a compromise."

"What kind of compromise?"

She leaned in and spoke softly. "Let me go for now. I can pay bail. The officers were impressed by the cash in my purse. In a couple of days, when you see I'm telling the truth, release the others." Mancini sat back and hummed as he considered his options. "Look, I'm about to make your career. Do you understand? If I'm lying, so what? One seductive whore got away. Big deal! But if I'm being straight, you'll be the next mayor of this city."

"You're good," Mancini acknowledged. "Very convincing." He was stalling for time. "If you want to become a C.I., a confidential informant, I'd have to talk to the D.A."

"Give me a piece of paper and a pen," she demanded. Seeing the expression on his face, she softened. "Please." He complied and she wrote down the vital information. "Be there at that time. You might want to bring the SWAT team."

"So I could end up the joke of the town?" But she did know about the call and the time it was made. "So it's not a lot of drugs. What is it? Firearms? Maybe Homeland Security..."

Sabrina began to tremble. "People," she replied. "Girls and women. From different parts of Asia. In large crates. Please save them!" Her dark eyes, moistened by tears, were shining like precious serendibite from the realms of Burma.

Mancini released a sustained whistle. "Women and girls in crates? Shipped like bulks of wheat?" He turned to Sabrina with fire in his face. "I swear, Sabrina! If you're lying to me, I will track you down. I'll plant more shit on you than you could carry! I'll toss you in a cell and lose the key!"

Sabrina put her finger to her lips. "Sssh. You're being recorded. Remember? May I see the girls before I leave?"

They left his office and Mancini told the cop he was taking her to holding. That pleased the cop, who returned to his own desk. But Sabrina was not being detained. She paid her bail with ease, and Mancini escorted her to the holding cell where the other girls were crying and shaking. Sabrina told them to be brave, to take care of each other. She promised them they would be OK in a couple of days. Once the girls were comforted, Mancini led her to a rear exit.

"Look, what you're asking," he noted. "I can't just give you a special exemption. If I make you a confidential informant, I have to go through the D.A." Sabrina squinted with distrust. "He's clean. I know the guy."

Sabrina grunted. "I also know a lot of guys. Nobody's all clean." Then, in a near whisper, she added, "Once this shipment is grabbed, the D.A. might want to give me an award. So don't worry about him."

Out in the street, nothing else was said between them. Sabrina scanned the scene, gave Mancini a quick glance, and disappeared into the shadows of the evening.

****

Barrett was close to giving up hope of getting any sleep. Sabrina's disappearance was like a trap door that dropped him into a pit of doubts and fears. A reality that had engulfed him was suddenly deleted; leaving one haunting memento: a ring of great value with ancient ethnic symbols etched into a valuable gemstone. Brin never seemed to fit the role she was playing but he knew so little about her life story. With pangs of regret, he wished he had probed further. But she always fielded his questions with cryptic replies.

After turning to his left, then his right, he laid flat and tried deep breathing. But the galloping noise in his head broke any moment of serenity. Yielding to insomnia, he slipped out of bed to not disturb Adrienne. His mouth was dry and raspy. He walked to the kitchen for a drink of water. Staring out the kitchen window, he watched an illuminated cloud pass over a waxing moon. Branches from an old oak tree scratched against the house. Something scurried across the deck, like a sudden thought that was too quick to capture into consciousness.

"What are you doing up? It's late." Barrett was startled by Adrienne who had entered the kitchen with stealth. Her tone sounded annoyed, critical; or maybe just tired.

"I know it's late," he snapped back at her. "I don't need a timekeeper." Seeing an expression of pain on her face, Barrett relented. "Sorry. I can't sleep. A lot on my mind."

She rubbed her eyes with her fingers and coughed. "What happened to the night job?" She grabbed a glass and also got a drink. "I guess you're used to being awake at this time."

"Yeah," he answered. "I guess that's it." A deep sadness covered him as the cloud had covered the moon. He decided to take a risk. "Adrienne, what happened to us?" It was an objective inquiry. "When did it go wrong?"

She finished her drink and rinsed out the glass. With a grunt, she sat down. "You want to talk...now?" It was her turn to stare out the window. The moon was starting to reappear as the cloud departed.

"Why not?" Barrett retorted. "The kids are asleep. It's quiet. No distractions." He slowly ran his hand through her hair. "Besides, it's long overdue."

Adrienne was bewildered by his sudden affection. "What's wrong, Barry?" She asked with true concern. "It's not just you and me, is it?"

He diverted the question. "Let's start with you and me, ok?" He sat down next to her and waited for some information.

Adrienne looked down to her fumbling fingers. "You're always annoyed at me, irritable."

"Me?" Barrett almost laughed at the sense of irony. "Really?" Then he checked himself. "Look, I don't want to fight. I guess we've both been on edge with each other."

"All right. Fair enough." Adrienne was more awakened. " I guess I ask the same question. We used to worship each other. Do you remember that? We wanted to share everything, and…be together."

"Yeah. I guess every relationship changes."

"This isn't just normal changes." Adrienne was revived and alert. "It's bitter and angry and hostile."

Barrett wanted to deny her portrayal but saw the truth in it. With his elbow on the table, he supported his head with his arm. "Yeah, it's been pretty wicked. Maybe having three kids did it." Then, with a deep sigh, he asked, "Was it the abortion?"

She shook her head. "No. I'm glad we agreed about that. If anything it was a relief. But it did signal the end of a time in my life." He saw the look on Adrienne's face, as if she were staring down a deep abyss.

"When did it break?" asked Barrett. "When was it all just another day?"

"We both went through big transitions around work," Adrienne reminded him. "I went from nurse to cosmetologist. You went from software programming to insurance sales."

Barrett let out a short laugh. "Neither of us ended up with the person we married, eh?"

Adrienne sighed. "Life plays tricks on us." She frowned and bit her lip. "I know I'm not as sexual as you may like." Barrett tried to wave that off but she persisted. "No, it's true. I'm frustrating you." She stared out at the moon that was again in full view. "I'm sorry. It's just not there for me any more."

"I know." He was sympathetic, eager to reassure her. "And if you try to do it just to please me…well…I know it."

They sat in silence and processed what was shared. A shadow rushed across their vision. "It's a mouse," declared Adrienne as she pointed toward the deck. "He visits at night. Just watch."

"Huh?" Barrett looked out the window. They sat patiently together. "Oh yeah," he whispered. "There he goes!" They both giggled. "I like this," he said. "It's playful. We haven't played much lately." She nodded in agreement and he took her hand. They sat like that for a while. It no longer mattered how long or what time it was. He pulled Adrienne close and she leaned onto his shoulder.

"What does he search for, every night?"

"Who? The mouse?"

"Yeah. He never leaves with anything, but he keeps coming back."

"Hmm." They watched the nervous rodent sniff around and then scamper out of sight, into the darkness.

He did love Adrienne. He cherished his family. Nothing should dismantle the fortress they had created. And yet, there were cracks in the foundation. Deep fissures of frustration were branching into the bedrock. When he looked at Adrienne, he saw the woman who had given birth to their three children. He saw the creases of life that were sculpted into her face: the residue of broken dreams, the scars from settling instead of soaring, the traces of disappointment and distraction. He felt a deep gouge of guilt tear into his nerves.

But, just as intensely, a wellspring of painful craving cut across him, like surgery without anesthesia. Sabrina: Her deep eyes and raven hair; the passion ignited by her touch; her calm confident understanding of his need; her joyful thrusting as they moved together in erotic synchronicity. Barrett admitted to himself, "I need her desperately." He was pulled in a futile tug-o-war, as he stroked

Adrienne lovingly while he fantasized about Sabrina. "I'm spread across two parallel universes. If I lose my balance, I could fall into endless space."

11

Nightmares and Rendezvous

When awake, she moves as if sleepwalking; but when asleep, the dreams are too real...

Whenever her work is done, or after Barry leaves, Sabrina slips into a reverie. Most of all, she misses her sister. As young innocent girls, they had dreams that were filled with hope and romance. But her sister dreamed only of meeting the perfect man and celebrating a wedding deep into the night. Sabrina had different dreams. She thought about becoming a teacher or a doctor. She thought about the European women who came to their village. They worked for an organization that was building schools and hospitals. Those women knew things Sabrina wanted to know.

When the two sisters did talk about weddings, they avoided questions about the wedding night itself. Their husbands would teach them those things. But how did the husbands know?

Sabrina remembered her first period. She was cramping and went to the bathroom. The blood frightened her. She went to her mother who slapped her, and then embraced her joyfully. It was a confusing message. Mother said she was ready to get married. Everything came rushing at her suddenly with no real explanation.

When Sabrina told mother she was afraid of marriage, mother told her not to worry; father would pick a good man for her. That answer did not soothe her. In fact, she became more anxious.

Her sister was eager to be married; but Sabrina wanted to go to school and become like those European women. Her head was filled with curiosity. She wanted to know about the world and the stars, the seasons and the weather. Why did water freeze or boil? How do new animals get born? What is love? She wrote poems nobody ever read.

Her sister's wedding was a marvelous affair. Eating, drinking, singing, and dancing through the day. The bride and groom would get to know each other in time. The families were happy with the financial negotiations. Many people told Sabrina, "You'll be next!" It was meant as a joyful acknowledgement; but Sabrina felt only a sadness that sank deep inside her.

She was seventeen years old when father told her he found the man for her. And he really was a man! He was almost forty years old and already married. The man's first wife suffered from a mysterious malady so they needed another woman for household chores. Sabrina protested and father demanded her respect. The argument escalated. Sabrina said the man should hire a maid. Father slapped her. Sabrina ran to her room. She was hurt, angry, frightened; but her spirit was strong. A fire burned inside her, something like a hunger that could not be sated. Sabrina knew her childhood was finished.

After a few months, her family gave up the search. Sabrina settled into another village and helped mothers with their large families. She always wanted to be a mother; but did not want to share the fate of the overburdened women with too many children. She didn't want the desperation she saw in their eyes. In her free time, Sabrina would read books that a friend brought her from the local library. She continued writing poems no one read.

Then one day in town, she met two couples her own age. They wore nice clothes and were enjoying an afternoon in a café. The women were also allowed at the cafe, as long as they remained at an outdoor table. In addition to a bottle of wine, the four friends shared a hookah that was set on the ground near them. Sabrina could smell the sweet aroma emanating from the smoke as they passed the nozzle around. They seemed to be visitors from another world, sophisticated and "cool". One of the men noticed Sabrina and whispered to his companion. They invited Sabrina to join them.

The wine, the smoke, and the easy-going conversation put Sabrina at ease. For once, she was among peers who could share a modern perspective on life. When they learned about her situation, they offered an enthusiastic alternative. "You'll work in an office. You'll get an education and good training." One of the women assured her, "You'll have your own money. You'll be independent."

Sabrina remembered her excitement as she anticipated a new life of freedom and respect. The next morning, the private car arrived right on time. With only a few personal items, she carried all her earthly possessions in two shopping bags.

The driver left the village and veered into a remote region in the mountains. Whenever Sabina inquired about their destination, the driver replied only, "Soon. We're almost there. Just relax." Sabrina noticed that he was perspiring even though the weather was chilly. They ascended upon a dusty encampment. Sabrina saw several trucks and a ring of quansom huts. They looked liked wrinkled soup cans on their side. The air was redolent of the kerosene that kept the huts warm. The driver led her to one of the huts. "Is this the office?" she asked nervously. "Sure," answered the driver as he pushed her toward the entrance.

When she entered the hut, her dream devolved into nightmare. Twenty cots were lined up in four rows. There were young women, in different stages of undress, on most of the cots. Some of them were crying and pleading, others were yelling, and others remained totally silent. Men and women, holding canes or small whips, were barking orders at them. One young woman, about Sabrina's age, shouted, "No!" to a woman and stood up. The woman shoved her to the ground and came down with her cane. A man rushed over. "Not her face," he shouted. "No need to damage the merchandise." The young woman sobbed heavily. "I want to die!"

On impulse, Sabrina turned to leave. The driver and two other large men restrained her. "Cooperate!" shouted one of the men. Sabrina's legs grew paralyzed and the men dragged her to one of the vacant cots. One man said to the other, "This one's hot." The other man replied with a guttural grunt. The driver said, "All the way, I was thinking about this moment." Then he added, "I'm pretty sure she's a virgin. Let me do it."

"No way. It's my turn. You know that."

"Yeah, but she's special. Next time, I'll let you go twice, OK?"

"All right. What the hell? It's never that different."

Sabrina was going far away, into one of her poems. She held onto one sentence: "She's special."

****

The nightmares always return, like an annoying relative that can't take a hint. She can actually feel the cold ground at her back, the powerful arms holding down her hands and feet. The driver is on top of her. She turns her head to avoid looking at his erect penis. He grabs her face and forces her to look. "Watch!" he commands. "Learn!" Another man, who seemed to be the leader, said, "Look at those eyes! She has eyes like a squirrel. All dark and squinty." She feels the penetration as the driver makes his plunge, tearing through her personal walls. She's screaming, not only because of the pain. She's stripped of all personal will.

In the regular assaults, Sabrina learned to separate from her body. The detachment helped her to survive. But in the nightmares, she's completely immersed in the experience. She knew it was necessary. She had to reclaim her body, re-engage with her sensation; remember all the details to boost her determination whenever she faltered in her mission.

Her eyes open wide as she escapes from the dream. Her body is soaked and her breath is rapid. Her heart is pounding like a bass drum in her chest. When she feels a hand at her arm, Sabrina turns with a jolt. It's Gizem.

Sabrina nods and sinks into Gizem's arms. The sophisticated woman, who confronts harsh realities of the world, is comforted by a precocious girl who's nine years old.

****

Gizem had done her part. The address in Sabrina's note brought him downtown to the western edge of the city. On a narrow block, cramped among tenements, cafes, churches, and bistros, the building, with its red brick façade rose over ten stories high. The entrance was announced with a stone archway and the door was locked. Barrett had to ring for entry and used the number mentioned in her letter. A scratchy voice came through the monitor. As instructed, Barrett gave his name and mentioned the ring.

When he was buzzed inside, Barrett was in an alcove with high ceilings. The floor branched out to several open studios. A ballet troupe was rehearsing in one loft while actors were stumbling over their lines at another that had been converted into a small theatre. Despite the high ceilings, he had to bend down to avoid a few overhanging pipes.

He found the room number and knocked at the door several times. In time a woman/man in a casual dress emerged. Except for a stubble of beard and a gruff voice, the feminine touches of makeup, hairstyle, and strut were executed with precision.

They left the hallway and entered a waiting area. The she-man closed the door and directed Barrett to have a seat. The queen adjourned to another room and Barrett was left in the dimly lit vestibule. Being in a strange building with a priceless ring, bearing nothing but an obscure letter, would try any one's patience. But he wanted answers to a dozen questions and he trusted Sabrina.

Three rather solid gentlemen entered the room. One by one, they shook his hand. Their firm grasps were impressive and intimidating. They were tall with athletic physiques and confident postures.

The man in the center spoke. "Good evening, Barrett. My name is Mutashim (decent, honest, modest). You have something for me?"

Barrett, in a hidden room in a remote building, was suspicious of every one and everything. "Excuse me, Mutashim. I need to see some identification."

Mutashim peered into Barrett's eyes. "You don't trust me?" he asked with a definite note of challenge. The other two made restless gestures.

Mutashim raised his hand and they settled down.

Barrett stood firm. "Why would I?" he countered. "We are strangers to each other."

"Very well," the Asian replied and slipped his hand inside his jacket. He could've been grabbing a gun. But he pulled a wallet with his driver's license and a gym membership. Both cards had his photograph. Barrett studied the documents but was still wavering.

The Asian discerned his predicament. "Sabrina sent you, eh?" Barrett's eyes opened wider. If he were a dog, his ears would've pointed to the man. "I don't need to see your I.D. Sabrina described you well."

"Alright then," replied Barrett. "What now?"

All three men laughed. "Now you show us the ring, of course," answered Mutashim.

Barrett reached into his inner coat pocket and pulled out a jewelry case. After studying the men one more time, he handed the ring to Mutashim.

He opened the case and the three men gasped in unison. Mutashim held the ring up to the light. One of the other men, who went by the name of Hadi (guide), took out an eyepiece and analyzed the ring. He nodded with a smile. But the third man, Laiqa (intelligent, smile), seemed unconvinced, and spoke as if arguing. But Mutashim quashed his skepticism with a strong rebuke. Laiqa shrugged and relented.

Mutashim smiled at Barrett. "Welcome friend. Come with us." He led the way through another door. They entered an atrium that was once an auditorium. A stage was at the front of the hall like a misplaced symbol from a different dream. About twenty desks were arranged in a circle. There was a laptop computer on each desk and the operators faced the center of the circle. They were all in eye contact every moment. Some shouted to others in the circle. Clearly, they were all part of a shared network.

Barrett was staring at the mobile computer center when he heard a woman's voice. "The best techies in world, Barry." He knew the voice intimately. Barrett turned. "Sabrina! What a relief." He embraced her eagerly and she held him with a firm clutch. They kissed happily.

He swept his hand around the circle. "What is this?"

Sabrina made a proud announcement. "You are looking at a small slice of the Seljuk Network of Hacking, Tracking, and Forging."

Barrett was fascinated. "Are you telling me there are cells like this all over the country?"

"Think bigger, Barry," she replied. "All over the world."

Barrett released a low whistle. "Homeland Security must be watching you. You guys fit the profile: Asians, a lot of Muslims, operating in small units."

"Everyone here is totally legit," replied Sabrina. "Besides, your Homeland Security is full of holes. They hire a lot of private contractors. Sometimes the traffickers get the jobs before we can embed someone."

Mutashim joined their conversation. "You see him?" He pointed to one of the operators. "He's a surgical oncologist in one of your major cancer centers. And that woman." He pointed to another desk. "A professor of Philosophy at a big university in this city."

Barrett was intrigued. "So they're all assimilated," he concluded.

"Yes," said Sabrina with enthusiasm. "But in good ways. We're not terrorists, Barry. We're revolutionaries. We admire your Founding Fathers and your Constitution. Not their slavery, of course."

Barrett grunted. "Of course not. You're the Abolitionists." He considered the implications. "During our Civil War, we fought eleven States and a couple of Territories. It was horrible. We lost over 600,000 lives. But you guys are fighting slavery today, throughout the whole world!"

Sabrina pursed her lips. "Yes. You now understand the magnitude of our crusade. Obviously, we don't use any known Internet service. Our techies created their own dark net."

Mutashim turned to Sabrina. "Why don't you give him a tour?" he suggested.

Sabrina walked Barrett around the circle. He watched fingers move rapidly over keyboards; and screens lit with telephone tracks, changing maps, dynamic graphs, and other numerous bytes of data. He saw several operators creating passports and visas with official stamps and lamination.

"It's all mobile," Sabrina noted. "We could be packed and gone in fifteen minutes."

"My god!" Barrett considered the reality he had entered. "An old landmark building with lofts and penthouse apartments. Next door, you have ballet recitals and Off Off Broadway theatre. In the middle of it all, a global network that penetrates and sabotages trafficking gangs and organizations. Incredible!" His old techie soul was sparked. "But what they're doing? Way out of my pay grade!"

"Remember," stated Sabrina. "Two hundred billion dollars a year. And only forty billion is sex slaves. Most is labor. The global economy is like your Old South!"

"With that kind of money, when salaries are squelched and living costs keep rising, corruption is very tempting. So you can't just go to official authorities."

"Exactly. That's why we had to test you like this."

Barrett recognized one of the operators. "Hey! I know you!"

"Uh huh," said the young man. "I met you a few times. I'm one of Sabrina's quote unquote customers. I was one of the hasty clients. I bet you thought I had issues."

"Yes, that's right." Barrett turned to Sabrina. "So you don't sleep with all your 'customers'. Some are network contacts?" The operator laughed and turned back to his screen.

Sabrina smiled and brushed his hair. "Correct, my dear. But I do have to earn a living." Barrett was slightly disappointed. She wrapped her arms around his neck. "I promise to always shower before we get together."

"Hmm." Barrett smirked playfully. "For the greater good, eh?" She giggled and sank into his chest. "The ring. It's so valuable."

"Priceless," she agreed.

Barrett grunted. "Couldn't you just give me a good replica? Did I have to run around with that priceless stone just to be tested?"

Sabrina smiled at him and tried to explain in simple language. "The first thing you did was get an appraisal, right?" He nodded. "If it was just a cheap bauble, you would've just tossed it in a drawer somewhere. But, if you realized it was very valuable, you would search for answers."

Barrett made some quick calculations. "You must be paying five thousand a month for this space. Quite a commitment! How did you find this building?"

Sabrina answered with casual efficiency. "Henry Anderson, the big real estate guy? He tried to buy it and end the rent protections. He wanted to convert the whole thing into super-elite condos."

Barrett sighed deeply. "The whole city is under attack by developers. The neighborhoods are disappearing. It's becoming all high-rise structures and gentrified businesses. The age of the bohemian is done."

Sabrina laughed sarcastically. "Not really. With the growing divide between the few 'haves' and the greater 'have-nots', we'll all have to learn bohemian survival."

12

The D.A.

District Attorney Richard Williams likes to maintain a casual style but leaves no doubt as to his legal abilities. He often dispenses with wearing a tie and will roll up his shirtsleeves for effect. But, on points of law, he can render the opposition dumbfounded. He loves to go after white-collar crime that, he often emphasizes, is not a victimless crime. For a man in his sixties, he looks good. He keeps a healthy diet and has a regular gym workout four days a week. He will consume some alcohol, but only at nominal levels. He likes to keep a clear head. His only real weakness, which his wife allegedly knows about but tolerates, is a penchant for "professional working women", his term for elite call girls. He discovered that the Eastern European professionals know how to remain discreet. This hobby placed him in a few intimate contacts with Henry Anderson, the real estate mogul, whose wealth buys a lot of influence.

He gave Detective Mancini's CI request the respect it deserved. "Listen, Sal, I like you personally and I know about your work on the Long Island case. The bodies of those young girls…" He paused to take an extra breath. There are times when even weathered enforcement agents can feel the trauma. "But this situation leaves a lot of red flags."

"C'mon. Rich." Mancini often grew impatient with Williams' caution that could delay a major operation. "Technically, she was arrested for a crime, so I gotta come to you. But the crime is part of her cover. And the crime got her to me. We vetted her. No priors on the record."

"Yeah. I hear you." The D.A. was honest but also a political animal. "But this is one of those CIs with OIA benefits. You want her to get C1 status."

"Of course." Mancini knew the DA's reputation and found his hypocrisy annoying. "OIA? Really? Otherwise Illegal Activity? She's a prostitute, sure. But it's the edge we need. But she has to maintain her income source. Hell, she paid her own bail, man!"

"Cash bail?" asked Williams, feeling some personal anxiety. "I hate using hookers to catch hookers," he noted. "It gets convoluted."

Mancini pushed his point. "Rich, we're not talking about a few brothels and pimps. The lady has access to a network of information."

"What are you saying? How big is this?"

"We should have proof of her reliability in a few days. She said it could make both our careers. Major organized crime."

"Whoa!" Williams had his out. "If it's that big, she's not a Confidential Informant. She's an Asset for the FBI."

Mancini's annoyance broke though into pure resentment. "If you bring in the Feds, this bird's gonna fly! She has to remain completely unknown to be effective. You know that!"

Williams interlocked his hands and studied Mancini. Since the Long Island serial killer case, the man had been on a crusade. He concluded that the Detective could be a political asset or a political enemy. If a large operation failed, Mancini would run him over the coals. But, if a major bust did occur, Williams would share the credit. "Right now she's on bail. Let's postpone the court appearance. We may want to keep her record clean. If this big operation really happens, I'll get her the CI status and let her continue her OIAs. Within clear limits. We got a deal?"

"Yeah, ok," Mancini frowned. "Those other girls?"

Williams laughed. "If she really cared about them, she'd pay their bail, too."

"The girls were our leverage. But only for a few days."

Williams snorted his reply. "Damn, Sal! Your bleeding heart is getting to me. ROR. Time served. Fair enough?"

Mancini shook his hand. "You're ok, Rich."

"Let's just hope this hooker is an honest lady, eh?"

When Mancini left, Williams thought about calling Henry Anderson. Some coded message might be in order. Williams liked the women; Anderson appreciated cheap labor for his building projects.

It's all one big circle. The gap between the super-rich and desperate masses keeps growing. The rich can sabotage labor unions and wage laws with covert labor. The poor get more desperate and fall into the web of trafficking just to feed their families. The angry worker, displaced by automation and business relocations, blames the hungry migrant for stealing jobs. The bottom-dwellers are at each other's throat while the oligarchy purchases more land and bigger yachts. Money can grease the wheels. When workers are hungry, they accept bribes with minimal regard for ethics and laws. The wheel keeps turning. Like a snowball down a hill, it's growing and its direction is out of control.

Williams picked up the phone but then reconsidered. He decided to wait and see how the lady's information played out before he involved any one else.

****

Sabrina suggested that we meet in the waiting area of an upscale lounge in midtown. I got to the address and was impressed by the chic atmosphere with subdued lighting and plush leather seats. The hostess who greeted me wore a long clinging evening gown of soft purple velvet. Her rich blonde hair fell beyond her shoulders and was infused with jeweled dots that sparkled in the glow of well-placed lanterns. I informed her that I was anticipating a date; so she guided me to the waiting area, which was worth a month's rent. I reclined on a comfortable sofa, sipped a cocktail, and took in the slow jazz that bordered on a meditation.

As I waited anxiously, Kenny arrived at the restaurant. Kenny, my boss, was not accompanied by his wife, but by a youthful Latina with a lot of flashy jewelry. He mentioned her name a couple of times: Sarita. Weird, I thought, one letter different than Sabrina. I turned away and buried my face in a menu. Of course, he'd be loath to be seen by me as well. So it's a furtive balance. Then again, if we did connect, we could gather for a covert joke. Fortunately, I didn't have to choose that option. He took his date to a discreet booth with low lights near the piano.

Sabrina materialized like an apparition and took my breath away. Hovering over me like a conquering warrior, she was wrapped in a low-cut style that concealed little. Her skirt of emerald green stopped at mid-thigh, teasing me with her perfect legs. Long jade earrings poked out from her raven hair like nervous birds. Just enough mascara enhanced the slant of her deep dark eyes. She had added hints of green tint to her hair. Her lips were painted in gentle amber but the polish on her long nails was blood red.

When I was able to breathe, I complimented her choice for our rendezvous. "Nice place. It's so obvious and yet so hidden. Just a waiting room."

She leaned in to whisper in my ear. The scent of her perfume and the tender zephyr of her breath sent a charge through me. I was subdued, a slave to her powers. "Are you ready to come with me?" she sighed. Silently, I nodded and rose from the sofa.

Passing by the hostess, I explained that, "Something's come up."

"I'll bet it has," Sabrina muttered as we departed from the lounge.

****

We did not go to her apartment that night. She said we had to be more discreet for now. That comment left me confused but, reflecting on all the factors involved, I played along without question. She hailed a cab and we arrived at a boutique hotel in Murray Hill. It didn't feel like a hotel at all; more like a comfortable apartment building with a doorman. Sabrina went to reception and got the key. It was all planned out precisely. Sabrina could see, from my posture and facial expression, that I felt diminished by her dominating the situation. She giggled and whispered, "Stop slumping your shoulders. You're the stud for the night, big guy." I relaxed, smiled, and straightened my stance.

"At least let me press the elevator button," I whispered back. We got to the ninth floor.

"Here," she teased as she handed me the key. "You can even open the door for me."

It was a nice room, tucked away in a quiet corner. The bed wasn't too firm. It gently yielded to my weight. I took out my wallet but she said, "No. No money. Not this time." Sabrina loosened her hair and removed her skirt. In her half-slip she mounted me and sank down to kiss, long and lovingly. Then she sat up and unbuttoned my shirt. The flat-screen TV also contained a digital music radio, which she clicked on to meditative jazz.

While she stroked my bare chest, she asked, "You want to know red tantric Buddhism?" I had previously told her about my research. "From India," she explained. "Of course, the celibate monks kept it out of their sutras." She put my hands on her breasts and started to grind in sequence with the music. "But it survived. The union of male and female energies, Shiva and Shakti, can also be sacred." She closed her eyes and floated with the serpentine undulation. "Animus, Anima."

She opened her eyes and stopped the movement. "Let's take a cleansing warm shower." She left the bed and removed the rest of her clothes. A bronze goddess in the dim light. I got out of the bed, stripped, and took her extended hand. "Later, I have a favor to ask of you."

The impressions still haunt my memory: the warm cascade, the soap, the slippery feel of her body, dripping hair, a sustained embrace, my fingertips on her nipples, her flat stomach leading to her heat. We wiped each other down with thick fluffy towels.

Back in bed, we sat up and wrapped our legs around each other. With practice, we synchronized our breathing. "Kundalini," she murmured. "Let the snake rise from your base." We began to rock in accordance with the natural polarity of the universe. "Up," she continued. "Through your core...to your heart...rise." Like waves in the ocean, the power of our fervor devoured us. "The monks focus on the rising Kundalini. But it actually oscillates, up and down. Up and down." I was on the verge of eruption. "Wait," she directed softly. "First, absorb Shakti from me." She took hold and inserted me inside her. "Breathe...Hold...Breathe...Hold."

A charge climbed through me. My mind was illuminated with a total radiation. Male/female, Man/Woman, Good/Bad, Sacred/Sin...All polarity vanished. There was no boundary between us or anything else. All life is a version of cosmic energy. She said something about "Brahma" and "beyond delusion" but the words no longer mattered. I began to sink into the mattress and she followed me down. "Stay inside me," she sighed. I lay there for an eternity with Sabrina on top of me. Gradually, the boundaries returned. We gently stroked each other and meditated on the throb of each other's heart. In time, we settled, side by side.

When the sense (or delusion) of "self" and "other" once again enclosed us, I was struck with a profound insight. "You're something very ancient, something I read about." Sabrina smiled knowingly. "A Sacred Prostitute."

Sabrina giggled. "Yes. The Whore of Babylon. Jezebel. Daughter of Devi. Veshya. The prophets condemned us; yet you still dance the hora!"

I took that in and felt a gush of fresh air run through my veins. The ghost of Calvin and the Puritans was flushed out of my system. Neurotic presumptions of sin were exorcized.

Sabrina leaned toward me. Her mood shifted to serious. "Now we have to talk about a favor I need." I sat up attentively. In anxious anticipation, I wondered if a cash payment would have been a better idea. "I need you to deliver the ring someplace." I grew alert but wanted desperately to keep trusting her. "I'll give you the address. Ask for a specific person by name. When you meet him, and only him, mention my name. When he let's you in, give him the ring."

She went to her purse and retrieved an envelope. "And give him this."

I tensed and grunted. "Was all this a set-up? What you're asking…is it dangerous? I need to know more…"

She jumped in to clarify. "I believe my apartment is under surveillance. That's why we came here. I am protecting you." She took my face in her hands. "I love you."

"I feel like I'm getting into something with little knowledge…"

Again she broke in. "Do you care about Gizem? Does she fascinate you?" Without hesitation, I nodded. "There is a crate full of Gizems arriving on a ship."

"A crate?" I asked in bemusement. "Like a big box?"

"Yes." She was serious and gave me time to comprehend the horror.

"Are you telling me that a large box of young girls is being delivered?"

Sabrina lowered her eyes. "About fifty girls and young women. They've been in the box for three weeks."

I sat up in shock. My jaw dropped. "My god! How did they survive? How did they…"

"They were given some food every day. For the toilet, they shared a large bowl."

After the ecstasy of our sacred loving, this information hit me like a locomotive. There was nothing I could say to cushion the jolt of this modern slavery. "Unbelievable!" was my pathetic reply.

"Will you help us?"

What human being could refuse? "Of course," I said.

She handed me the envelope and took my hands. "Thank you, my love." She kissed me. "One more thing."

"There's more?" I asked as I stared at the envelope.

"Gizem," she replied. "She needs a sanctuary. A safe house. She also needs to be in a regular education. So far, she's been home-schooled and she's very smart. But it's time to get her assimilated. I have all the necessary papers."

"Brin," I queried. "Are you asking me to adopt Gizem?"

13

The Cargo Arrives

T he merchant ship arrived at the urban harbor carrying its covert cargo. With its wide berth, the ship's bow cut through the rough current with ease. Blowing the loud horn, the vessel pilot steered skillfully into its designated bay. On deck, in front of the bridge, large steel crates were stacked up to five or six high. The ship bore the flag of Panama; but it was only a flag of convenience. After the ship was moored, powerful cranes rose to their full height. On the dock, a flatbed lorry drove parallel to the ship.

One by one, the operator of the crane lifted a steel crate and placed it on the lorry, until four crates were loaded on the truck. Several officers, stationed along the dock, peered through binoculars and made cell phone calls. When they located the trap doors on the crates, they confirmed that the information was valid.

Once the lorry left the busy pier and proceeded on the open road, federal and state squad cars materialized with lights flashing and sirens blaring. The passengers in the lorry realized they could never evade such a detachment. They pulled onto a remote exit and came to a quick stop near a town park. Abandoning the truck, they ran into the woods. Several agents pursued the transporters while the rest of the team approached the lorry.

A federal officer found the trap door and tapped on it with his rifle. "Hello? Are you OK in there? You're safe now. I'm from the FBI." A United Nations agent approached another crate and called into the trap door. Dogs were called to sniff the crates in case they were booby-trapped. It was known to happen. If their cargo was intercepted, the ghouls might blow up the "commodities". After cautiously examining the boxes with heat sensors, the agents opened the crates and, with flashlights, peeked at the cargo.

Frightened girls and stoic young women, traumatized into silence, were huddled against the walls. Girls were clinging to the older females, forming a mass of terrified humanity. Slowly, the female UN reps entered the crates and drew near the precious captives. The smell emanating from the container was overwhelming. It was from the bowl used as a common toilet.

No one in the TV room had a dry eye as the trembling victims emerged from their steel captivity. Adrienne leaned against Barrett and sobbed. "How terrible!" she groaned. Candice sat with her knees bent into her chest and her eyes glued to the TV. Glenn turned to Barrett. "Dad, what are they gonna do with those little girls?"

Adrienne was at a loss but Barrett tried to keep it simple and insulated. "They treat them like slaves. They make them work for people."

"What kind of work?" asked Glenn.

"Whatever people need them to do," replied Adrienne curtly.

Glenn leaned in toward Barrett and whispered. "Like in those videos? The little girls?" His tremulous voice conveyed pure horror. Barrett nodded silently. "I wish we had some super-heroes," he mumbled.

"Indeed," said Candice sarcastically. "Wonder Woman or Supergirl."

"That's enough, Candi," Adrienne ordered.

Barrett stared at the unfolding news before his eyes. "I had something to do with that," he realized silently. "How do I turn away now?"

The second half of the report involved rehabilitation efforts. Some of the young women were placed in shelters that were run by

NGOs and religious organizations. Barrett was deeply moved when he watched the transformation from traumatized victim to serious student or sociable friend. Of course, some of the young women remained withdrawn, guarded, and non-verbal. It was to be expected. They'd need extensive counseling and support services.

The final fifteen minutes involved the customers, the men who were rounded up in trafficking networks. The meeting occurred in a large auditorium. The woman interviewing the men was fairly attractive herself, probably in her late thirties, with long blonde hair and a slender figure. To protect the privacy of the men, each one got a black ski mask to conceal his face. The effect was to make them look malevolent, evil, threatening. As the men replied to standard questions, Barrett and his family learned they ranged in age from the twenties to over eighty. Their occupations were just as diverse, from skilled professionals to manual laborers. They were evenly divided between married and single.

The woman interrogated one of the johns. "You're married. You have children. You have a good job. Why did you do this?" Barrett joked to himself, "Hah! Because he was married with kids and a demanding job," he thought privately. But the john simply answered, "I have an addiction." The woman moved on to a younger guy, single, who had girlfriends. He gave the same answer, "I have an addiction." The show ended with the impression that the men who paid for sexual services were all sex addicts.

Tucked away in bed later that night, Barrett was left with his own thoughts. Addiction? The answer did not settle with him. Of course, addiction is a disease of denial. But still, couldn't there be more than one reason? Barrett loved Adrienne and his children. He worked hard to maintain their lifestyle and support the kids through college. Nonetheless, what he felt for Sabrina was sincere, deep, and pure. An addict uses booze or other drugs to numb feelings or escape from the stress of life. His episodes with Sabrina were certainly an escape. Those moments of total release rendered him malleable. But his relationship with Sabrina was also a restoring palliative. He was able to cope and adapt to whatever was thrown at him. He was less irritable with Adrienne's moods, more patient when Glenn acted like a jerk or Candice played the role of deplorable teenager. He had greater perspective and tended to no longer over-react to minor annoyances. Chuck's obnoxious jokes just rolled off him. Kenny's jabs didn't penetrate very deep. In other words, his relationship with Sabrina rendered him more functional. Does an addiction accomplish that?

****

The late-night press conference was aired over all the major networks. The Mayor gave an impassioned speech with the Chief of Police at his side. With lights flashing and cameras clicking, he pounded on the podium to emphasize his administration's unwavering opposition to any kind of human trafficking. Several reporters shouted out questions and the Mayor turned the podium over to his Chief to summarize the steps in the waterfront intervention. The microphone was then turned over to Detective Salvatore Mancini from Vice. He was a man in his early fifties who had wanted Homicide but settled for Vice. Writing up under-age drinkers, interrogating trembling drug addicts, and violating bars for being careless with phony IDs from the young crowd, were not his preferred missions in life. But, over time, he had made a lot of friends, did people enough favors, looked the other way when he could, and nurtured a decent reputation on the street. With a salary around eighty grand a year, it was always tempting to accept a few "gifts" and let low-grade perps walk away; but Mancini had a nose for trouble and maintained a clean sheet with the department.

"Good evening, Mayor. Thank you, Chief." Mancini faced the crowd with a cool that was cultivated over his time on patrol plus the last five years with his gold badge. He knew today's hot news was soon forgotten. The brief celebrity of a good grab didn't faze him. "This was a complex and well-organized apprehension. It required the cooperation and teamwork of many people. Although trafficking is a global crime, our community of dedicated public servants will never give it an easy welcome in our town." Even the objective reporters joined the rest of the audience in a round of applause. "There is no superman, no one hero, in this operation. The hero is the New York Police department and all the people who gave us their trust and their support. To the entire network that opposed this barbaric enterprise, I say thank you." One more round of strong applause. As the main players left the stage, the press secretary was left to field additional questions.

While they were escorted to the government limousine, the Mayor spoke discreetly to Mancini. "Should I be worried about my job? You gonna run for Mayor in the next election?" Mancini smirked and shook his head. "No way, Your Honor. You can keep Gracie Mansion. It's too draughty for me." The Mayor let out a deep guffaw and countered with, "How about Borough President then?"

****

The European with a heavy accent watched the press conference with bleary eyes and a tense jaw. He picked up his untraceable burner phone and speed-dialed. An Asian answered. "Yeah. I saw it."

"This hurts. Supply ain't gonna let this slide." Europe was breathing heavily. "The money, the time, the effort, the favors...all lost. "

"You call any one else yet? No? Good. Something's goin' on in the Asian network. First, all the brothel busts, now this. Those girls are gonna talk. Even their daddies who sold them are in trouble. They're not gonna trust us. We need to set up a meet."

"Don't worry about those girls. The moles will talk to them. They'll be worried about their families if not themselves. They know what happens to rats. They've seen it with their own eyes."

"Yeah. Right now, they're just scared. When they get to the safe houses…"

Europe needed more data to take action. "You know anything about this Detective Mancini?"

"Not much," replied Asia. "Used to be a street cop, then got Vice. He's pretty clean, too. Not easy to tap. Maybe we could hack him."

Europe laughed with a sarcastic twist. "Kompromat? Just because I have a Soviet background, you think I'm the KGB! What about you, Asia? You still readin' Mao's little red book?"

"Hey, the Cold War's over. I'm just saying he wouldn't be the first Vice cop to have a kiddie porn collection."

"Sure, they'll buy that. Dumb. Why don't we just plant drugs in his car?" Europe growled in disgust. "So we set up the meet?"

"Yeah, in storage."

****

"You're usually better than this," Sabrina observed. "You're not surrendering this time. You're being a tense lover."

I got defensive. "If I wanted judgment, I'd stay home. It's cheaper."

Sabrina was too smart to buy that. "Really?" was all she needed to say. Her expression, a playful mocking, was all that was necessary. I couldn't hide from her. My shield melted in the heat of her empathy.

"Sorry, Brin. Yeah, I'm tense. Agitated. Too unsettled." She listened attentively. "I'm thinking about that damn video."

"About trafficking?" I nodded. "It's a typical orientation video."

I tried to avoid her gaze. Her eyes were like an x-ray into my core. "I don't like the way she interviews the guys. They're johns, they're customers. Just like me. She tells them to wear ski masks. It makes them look creepy." I find the courage to look straight at her. "Am I creepy?"

Sabrina lets out a gasp and then chuckles. "Of course. You're a dirty, creepy old man!"

"Sabrina! I'm serious!"

"I know," she replied. "But it's silly for you to think that way. The way we make love, we are so tender with each other. When the passion builds, we're both in it all the way. Not creepy. Sacred!" She takes my face in her hands, and moves me to her lips. Her kiss is always sweet.

But I can't find comfort. "The men are all ages, from twenty-something to eighty. All kinds of professions: programmers, counselors, dentists, lawyers, brokers, truck drivers, construction workers, retired. All different marital situations: single, engaged, married, separated, divorced, widowed. When she asked them why they pay a prostitute, they all give the same answer: 'I have an addiction'. It seems rehearsed, programmed." Then, somewhat cautiously, I ask, "Do I have an addiction?"

Sabrina cursed under her breath in some alien dialect. Selijuk? Turkish? Persian? Arabic? Chinese? I had no idea. "Stupid video," she carped with firm annoyance. "I guess the puritans made that one."

"What do you mean?"

"Religious Right, Evangelical fanatics. They turned an educational video into a public shaming. Those poor men! They all think they're sex addicts!" She took a few breaths to calm down. "These Evangelicals are spreading all over Asia; in Mongolia and China, and Korea. You find them in Thailand and Vietnam and Cambodia and Laos. They're growing in Malaysia and Indonesia. Even India! The men were intimidated, bullied. So they went along with their captors." With a grunt, she added, "Missionaries! Their good work is always mixed with brainwashing!"

I was surprised by her sympathy for the johns. "After everything you've experienced, you feel bad for the guys?"

"Of course," she replied. "I love men. The sensitive, kind, loving men. Men are really very sensual and esthetic. That's why women, with clothes, and hair, and makeup, can handle them so easily. They're suckers for beauty." She cursed some more and continued. "Such a stupid question to ask a man in that situation! What would she expect him to say, eh?"

I was intrigued by her bitter reaction to the so-called puritans. "I guess the religious right is bad for your business, too?"

With a sneer, she gave a sarcastic reply. "There is an old saying: 'Missionaries come to do good, and they end up doing very well.' Their impact is a double-edged sword." I listened intently, waiting for her to continue. "They condemn the Triple Goddess as a demon and then sell us their Trinity! They tell us their bible stories while turning every pleasure into sin. Sure, they build schools. But will those schools teach our children about evolution, the Big Bang, quantum physics? Instead of science they indoctrinate us with ancient superstitions. Instead of Biology, we get Original Sin. Ah!" She waved her hand in disgust. "During an AIDS crisis, they preach Abstinence and prohibit condom use! We don't need more fundamentalisms. We need an Asian Enlightenment." Her indignation was pure.

"Yeah, I get that. The Age of Wisdom put an end to the religious wars in Europe. Before then, a mere difference of opinion could get you burnt at the stake or hanged or buried alive."

Sabrina's response blew me away. "Sartre was right. Being and Nothingness. The human is an ape that evolved a consciousness. Like trying to comprehend infinity, we're left with this existential void. We are mortal natural animals. If we can't accept it, we get very anxious. We search for meaning beyond the universe of natural laws. Our faculties fail us, so we create myths. Like a child's fairy tale, the myth comforts us. A god is watching. If we follow the god's rules, we'll be OK. We're safe in the god's embrace. No matter how many times that god fails us, we cling to the belief. It's a compensation for our limitations. Any one who has a different idea becomes a threat to our psychological stability. We are forced to face the Nothingness again. We are anxious again. So that person who dares to question or disagree is an 'infidel', a 'heretic', who must be destroyed.

I liked her reply, but doubts remained. "Brin, am I contributing to the problem? Am I part of the trafficking?"

She shook her head fiercely. "Not at all, my love! You saw the news report. You saw those girls rescued from those damn shipping crates. You took a chance, you trusted me, and you went into a strange neighborhood and delivered the message. You helped to free them!"

"I'm a father of three great children. I'm married. What I do with you could cost me my family and my job! Isn't that an addiction? I'm doing something that could have bad consequences."

Sabrina grew impatient. She pushed me back onto the bed and mounted me. Then she lowered her face toward me. "The group of men covered every age and every profession. Is it an addiction or a powerful need that is not being met?"

I ran my hands through her dark soft hair. I brushed my finger across her lips. "True. But addiction is also a need."

"Barry, are you raping young girls? Are you forcing a woman to do things against her will? Are you kidnapping, hitting, or whipping any one? Are you keeping any one prisoner with almost no food? Are you misrepresenting yourself, lying, to trap an innocent virgin?" To each question, I answered with a strong "No!"

"Have you paid me a fair amount? Have you followed my directions and let me lead? Do you respect me when I have to postpone any meeting? Do you provide a service to protect me?"

To those questions, I offered a sheepish, "Yes".

"The women are taken from Eastern Europe and Asia and Africa," she added. "In Africa and Asia, they are used mostly for slave labor. Most of the sex work is in Western Europe, the United States, and Japan. A forty billion dollar sex business. What do you think of that?"

"I'm not sure," I replied.

"Something in Western culture and Western marriage is breaking down. Your modern Western societies require people like me, eh?" That was hitting home for me. "You are a man with healthy needs. My service just fills a real need."

I pondered that. "So here we are in the West, with our sexy music videos, skimpy clothes, open conversation about sex, premarital relations, and yet..."

Sabrina finished the sentence for me. "And yet, you feel a lack, an emptiness in your loving. With all your appearance of being sexy, you need our endless supply. That's half the problem."

That last sentence hooked me. "Oh? What's the other half?"

Sabrina's expression was wise, and perhaps condescending sympathy. With a soft smile and a nod, she continued. "Before your country had its Civil War, the southern states had an elite that led an elegant life. The plantation owners had the best manners and etiquette. But they could only maintain their style of living if they used slaves. Now, your labor unions are neutralized, the wealthy control the tax regulations, the rest are working two jobs just to pay basic bills. Your homelessness is on the rise. Your healthcare is a mess. Any time a progressive phase threatens the elites, the system snaps back. Don't you see?"

Enlightenment! "Are you saying we still need slavery to maintain our economy?"

"Precisely. The sex slaves fill your biological needs. The work slaves, over sixty per cent of the traffic, fills your economic needs. The West is still exploiting the Third World, Barry, but not with battleships and tanks. Even in your own country, you are becoming slaves to the master class. You fight for a few extra crumbs while the rich have lives you can't even imagine! Luxury homes are raised in a city where your teachers and plumbers and social workers can't afford the rent. Such a system cannot sustain itself without slaves." I wondered if Sabrina ran eloquent orientation seminars.

"Sonofabitch!" I felt relief roll through me as the tumor of guilt was excised. "It's not those poor johns who have an addiction. It's the powerful with their pornographic levels of wealth. They're addicted to money; they can't accumulate enough! And the rest of us, we may have our TV shows and our techie toys; but we're on a plantation!"

Sabrina reclined next to me. I relaxed and drew her face to mine. We kissed with no further regard about right or wrong. Our only focus was on the wonderful, glorious, orgasmic moment we were sharing.

14

A Dark Meet

A storage facility, with its twenty-four hour access, was a good place for a meeting. Four inconspicuous cars approached the main entrance at a carefully staggered schedule. Each driver supplied a different entry code and the main gate rattled open each time. Once inside the planned sector, a metal gateway was unlocked and lifted like a window curtain. The light for the vault was switched on and four men entered the vacant enclosure. The gateway was then pulled down to hinder monitoring devices. The carefully controlled airflow was optimum for storage, and comfortable for concealed meetings. The men spoke in hushed tones so that piped-in music would block any recordings.

A stocky man with an eastern European accent started the conversation. "OK, what do your guys know?"

The Asian was the first to answer. "There has to be a rat at the supply side, because we all get hit."

The Arab considered that. "Yeah. But maybe we have a leak at the common target points. The docks, the airports."

Europe spoke again. "What do we know about this Detective Mancini? He's always in the right place."

Asia nodded. "Hmm. We can't touch him and don't even try. He's a Boy Scout. Obviously, he has good sources." He paused to bite his lip. "He's one of the cops who investigated those bodies in Long Island. You know, the young hookers? It changed him."

The Arab added a few pieces of information. "He's been in Vice about five years. He wasn't happy about it, wanted Homicide. But lately, he's really been into it. He grabbed a few liquor licenses from our strip clubs; under-age drinking shit. Why get so hot about that?"

"Maybe that Long Island case, eh?

"Sending a message?"

"Yeah, maybe," replied the Arab. "To who? What?"

The Asian answered nervously. "To us, man! He's sending a warning." He turned to the Arab. "Those bars? Were they big into the trafficking?" The Arab nodded. "Yeah." He paused to consider. "After they trapped my shipment on the pier, Mancini made a lot of news. Then the bars were hit"

Europe chirped in. "How did he know we diverted from Atlanta?"

"Who know?" The Arab shared a few more tidbits. "He's married to a woman who has a kid from her first marriage. The boy's in his twenties and just drifting. Maybe he's the weak link."

The fourth man, a Latino, who had been silently listening, joined the conversation. "So, let's keep it simple. We follow Mancini, we get to know his contacts." The others listened intently. "He works with a lot of business people, he brings in a lot of hookers and pimps. We keep notes, make a list."

"Yeah," said Europe. "We learn the patterns. We decide who the best possibilities are. We find out more about this step-son, too."

"That's right," Latino concurred. "Then we plant a test."

"Look," added the Arab. "We don't always get along. But, sooner or later, we're all accountable, right?"

Asia gave him a side-glance. "So what are you sayin'?"

"This is big. There's something working against us and it's not the damn United Nations! And the NGOs ain't organized enough for what's happening. We gotta trust each other now, work together, share everything we find out."

"I agree," replied the Asian. "We don't fight over territory right now." He looked around at the others. "But we also don't take advantage of the situation."

Europe nodded knowingly. "OK, I hear you. We'll settle the Brooklyn thing later."

"And the Lower East Side," added Asia.

"Hey," the Arab interjected. "We all have enough customers. So nobody be stupid."

Hands were shaken all around. The gateway was raised. One by one, they staggered from the storage chamber. No one would ever check the security cameras unless an incident occurred. For the rest of the night, there would definitely be no incidents around that facility.

****

Brian Murphy felt like the luckiest guy in the world. He was having a good time with the girl who drifted into his life a month ago. He was worried about the amount of alcohol they consumed during that month; but, hell, they were young. The last night was a blur of alcohol, pot, loud music and dancing. Fortunately, they didn't drive their own cars. He thought that, maybe, they called Uber.

Gina had made it so easy. She slid over and sat on the barstool next to him. They made some idle chatter, laughed at a few jokes, and shared some interesting life experiences. After a few drinks, she said, "I like you, Brian. Come home with me." It was very swift progress to the next level and he was taken aback. "What's wrong?" she teased. "You a male chauvinist? The guy has to make the move?" Skillfully challenged, he demonstrated his enlightened worldview by jumping in a cab with her.

He continued to doubt his reality when she basically assaulted him in her apartment. He was impressed by her skill in undressing him while he cautiously stroked her hair or rubbed her shoulders. She was soon kissing him liberally in most regions of his body. At some point, he decided to just let things happen, whatever it might mean.

A month later, he was very comfortable with Gina and eagerly anticipated their frequent rendezvous. Two weeks back, he asked, "Gina, are we just sex objects for each other?" He was plagued by that thought for a while. "I mean, we're all over each other. But I hardly know anything about you."

Gina's reply was not helpful. "Maybe. You're a man, I'm a woman. And we're having a good time. So don't think about it too much."

Brian would've liked to talk with his Dad about it. But their relationship wasn't like that. He wondered if Sal, his stepfather, could offer advice; but they had argued over Brian's life goals. Basically, he didn't have any. He expected more criticism from Sal about his wasting time. If his mother learned about his drinking binges, she'd go ballistic. She's hyper-sensitive to alcohol issues. Mr. Murphy had degenerated into an arrogant drunk and demolished their marriage. So, with no easy confidante to reach out to, Brian rode along on automatic pilot and enjoyed the ride.

Brian was wrecked when he woke up. The dim morning sun felt like a glaring fireball for him. Since he had no plans for the day, he thought about just staying in bed. Gina rolled around and wrapped her arm around him with a harsh swing. She grumbled and rubbed her eyes. "What time is it?" she groaned. When Brian told her, she groaned again.

"What happened last night?" she griped. "Did you have sex with me?"

Brian laughed. That was like asking if the sky was blue. "I don't know," he quipped. "Probably."

Her tone grew stern. "Did you fuck me when I was unconscious?"

"What? No. I wouldn't do that. I don't think so. I mean, you know, we were really wasted." He couldn't believe the nymphomaniac was accusing him of some kind of sexual violation.

"I don't believe it," she added. "You took advantage of me. You raped me!"

Brian couldn't believe how his partner in passion was turning on him. "No way, girl! Come on! That doesn't make sense."

She grew more sullen and turned away from him. "Could you just go," she pronounced. He was dazed and locked in silence so she added emphasis. "Get out! It's my place. Leave!"

"Really?" It was like someone had abruptly changed the TV channel.

She was adamant. "What do I have to do? Shoot you? Go!"

He tumbled around the bedroom as he gathered his clothes. "I'll call you later," he managed to vocalize.

"Get out!"

The world was spinning as Brian descended the stairs for the subway. Feeling off balance, he kept clear of the ledge and remained seated on a bench until the train arrived. The rattling and screeching of the ride was barely tolerable. How could such a powerful bond shatter like fragile glass? He again thought about telling Sal. After all, he's a cop and he knows the law. But he was reluctant to reveal more than necessary. "I always figured she was a little crazy," he concluded. "I guess this is how it ends."

****

Gilbert sat in the waiting area with Amanda. He insisted on escorting her to the interview. "I don't trust these agency types very much," he had quipped.

"I guessed you wouldn't mind sitting there with all the gorgeous prospects," she noted.

His reply was serious. "It's not like that. I just want to add some objectivity. There're a lot of con artists out there."

"You're sweet," replied Amanda with a kiss on his cheek.

They watched the other females waiting to be seen. Most of them were slender and they appeared nervous, twitching frequently, as they grasped their portfolios.

"I bet they're on uppers," whispered Gil. "Diet pills, ya know?"

Amanda grunted and handed him a lingerie catalogue. "Here! Enjoy yourself." A woman with a bright smile and excellent posture called her name and then guided her through a door to the initial interview.

Gil quickly grew bored with fashion magazines and found several computer journals on his cell phone. For fun, he searched "The Perfect Fashion Model" and was sent to an article on the common characteristics of the successful ones. Amanda met most of the statistics. She was tall enough and slender enough to fit the weight levels. Most models had agents but some women got lucky without one. Interesting facts about lighting and shading intrigued him. Although most pictures were brush-stroked or photo shopped, the women with natural clear complexions were preferred. He was surprised to learn how much skill went into proper posing for the shoots.

Amanda re-emerged with the smiling woman and was aglow. She had made it to level two. She would next face a screening in a different location. Gilbert wondered about the driving directions until Amanda told him she would be transported in the company's private car.

"It's out of town for privacy," Amanda explained. "A lot of famous models work there so they have to avoid the crowds. They also want to prevent a lot of paparazzi sneaking pictures."

Gil insisted on going with her. Amanda resented his intrusion but appreciated his caring. "So, how does Irene know these guys?" he inquired.

"I think they met at a party," she replied.

"What kind of party?

"Stop the Inquisition, will you! A business party I guess. OK?"

"Did they request nude photos?"

"Stop being so silly, Gil," she snipped at him. "But there may be some bikini shots."

"That settles it. I'm going with you."

She sighed in resignation. "Whatever."

15

Nightmares Linger

I t started as playful post-coital wrestling. We teased each other with provocative jibes and then tussled around the bed. Giggling and growling, we took turns assuming the top position. But then I rolled Sabrina onto the mattress and held her wrists. The mood changed in a flash.

"No! Don't do that!" She started to cry and her body quivered. I was startled when she began to plead pathetically. "Please let me go," she whimpered.

I quickly released my grip and looked down at her with concern. "What happened? What's wrong? Did I hurt you?"

Sabrina looked up at me for an arduous juncture in time. Her gaze was focused on someplace else. I dismounted and reclined next to her, waited patiently, and stroked her forehead.

"You can't imagine everything that happened to me," she finally whispered. "They held me down like that, my arms and legs…" She broke off.

"It's OK," I assured her. "You don't have to share everything."

She turned to her side and faced me with severe intent. "Yes I do! I have to purge the whole thing. The only way beyond the pain is through it. I trust you, Barry. I need you to know." Her words demolished any reservations I still retained. Love sewed us together.

"You like my tattoo? The Kundalini?" she asked. The question seemed to come from a different zip code. I could only answer with, "Yes".

She pointed to her hip. "Take a closer look at the snake." She guided me to the coiled base of the image. "Run your fingers across that part."

I did as she instructed and realized that part of the base was raised. "Look closer. Right there." On close inspection, I discovered that the tattoo was covering up a scar.

"I tried to conceal it," she explained.

"What is it?" I asked but I was filled with apprehension that she would tell me.

"Remember, it's slavery," she replied. "They mark their property. By then, I didn't care any more. I just begged them to not hurt me any more. They held me down, to immobilize me. I can still hear the roar of that propane torch. Oh my god, it was so hot! It burned. I never screamed like that in my life!"

I thought I was immune from all the horrors she had shared. But I felt pins and needles run through my legs and chest. I also wanted to scream. Instead, I stammered. "They…branded…you?" She nodded and I embraced her. "I'm so sorry."

"I don't want to hate any body," she said. "I want to get past the pain and the hate. Please, Barry, if you ever change your feelings about me, just be kind."

I held her and we rocked. "Oh, Sabrina! You always worry about me changing."

"Everything changes," she murmured. "Passions fade. The glaciers melt. Animals go extinct. Families sell their children."

All I could do was hold her and let time do its thing without us.

****

Adrienne came home to a quiet house. The kids were in the TV room. Glenn was finishing a homework assignment while Candice was lounging on the couch and sharing the latest gossip. The drama on the TV served merely as white noise, a filter that kept them focused on other things.

Candice looked up from her phone when her mother entered the room. Adrienne wore a demure black dress and minimal makeup. "Was it very sad, Mom?"

Adrienne wore a wistful expression. "Well, funerals are always sad. But she had a full life with a lot of love in it. So people celebrated her life." Adrienne fluffed Glenn's hair while he poured over a math problem. "You guys eat?" They grunted in the affirmative. "OK. I wanna take a shower and change clothes."

In her bathroom, she undressed and slogged into the shower. She felt the need to wash something undefined from her skin. She thought about Margaret, a woman in her late eighties who had a passionate history. She outlived three husbands, had several lovers and four children, and worked as a seamstress. Reportedly, she could throw back her share of whiskey. The woman lived through a World War; saw all the modern changes, had her share of loss, but managed to celebrate a joy in living. "Nevertheless, she died alone," thought Adrienne.

Margaret's children seemed to handle it well. After the solemn dedications, they seemed to enjoy the gathering for dinner. They joked with relatives and hugged friends. "I guess they inherited Margaret's joy," Adrienne concluded. She lathered up with shampoo and rubbed her scalp furiously. "Out damn spot!" Ruth and her husband, the Doctor, made an obligatory visit and said all the correct things. The Doctor asked about the diagnosis. Ruth shared an old Jewish saying: The song ends but the melody remains. Nice. But their behavior seemed rehearsed, like actors in a too-familiar play. Tabitha enjoyed the buffet but let me know that Margaret made an impact on her. Sarita's appearance was in contrast to her usual flair. Very minimal, no flash, taciturn. As usual, Sarita made a remark that cut deep. "All the makeup in the world is only denial. The truth is mortality."

Adrienne talked softly to her own reflection in the mirror. "When you were a nurse, you witnessed death many times. You had enough. You changed to cosmetology to escape, to cover up aging and mortality." The insight came in a jolt. "Now I'm trying to wash away death. If I don't stop, I'll cause serious abrasions." She shut the water and wrapped herself in a large towel. "Getting older is nobody's fault."

16

Pieces Come Together

S abrina chose the restaurant familiar to Barrett. He found her at
a table in a dark corner. Candlelight flickered across her face
and caused her eyes to glimmer when she looked toward him with a
smile. As he approached the table, Barrett noticed another
gentleman with her. The man rose when Barrett reached the table.

"Good evening, Barrett." Sabrina's tone was formal. She used
his full name. It put Barrett on guard. "I'd like to introduce you to
Detective Salvatore Mancini."

"Detective?" Barrett shook his hand. "How are you?"

"Please, gentlemen, be seated." Sabrina was confident, poised.
"We're all on the same side." They sat down. "I'm expecting another
guest. But we can start without her."

"OK, Sabrina, I've humored you this far." Mancini wanted to
regain some control of the situation. "Why are we here?"

"It's always been a convenient venue for Barry and me," she
replied. "It's time for you men to meet."

Barrett was on thin ice and chose to remain silent. Mancini was
less patient. "Really? And why is that?" demanded the Detective.

"You two live on the same block," replied Sabrina. "There's
nothing remarkable about two guys from the same neighborhood

meeting at the local bar, right?" Barrett felt a jolt go through him when she made that remark.

"So?"

"So I trust you both. Communication should be smooth."

"I see." Mancini glanced at Barrett. "You're her messenger?"

"First I heard about this," replied Barrett as he glared at Sabrina.

"I have to keep messages to a minimum," she explained. "Sorry, Barry."

"Ah! Here she is," proclaimed Sabrina as a young woman came to their meeting. "Gentlemen, this is Gina. She's Brian Murphy's friend."

Mancini's jaw dropped. He eyeballed the young woman with a tense jaw and rapid breath. "What the hell is this?" he roared.

"You wanna answer that?" Sabrina asked Gina.

"I could yoose some vater," replied Gina cautiously. Her accent sounded like somewhere in the Baltic. "And maybe some brandy." Sabrina signaled the waiter who took care of her request. "I know your son," she noted.

"My stepson," Mancini corrected. "You cried rape."

"Yeah, I did," she agreed. "They wanted to get to you."

"Who?" asked Mancini with fists on the tabletop.

Sabrina intervened. "She can't name names. Let her finish."

Gina nodded to Sabrina. Then she turned to Mancini. "After the Long Island case and the big bust at the pier, they have to tap you, throw a scandal at you."

"So they set up my stepson?" asked Mancini with rising anger. "And you were the bait?"

"We bailed her out," stated Sabrina. "Now she's a good guy."

Gina lowered her eyes. "I dropped the charges. I told them I was drunk. I said it was consensual. But now I'm scared."

"You have here a witness cooperating with you against their network. She needs protection now."

Mancini was suspicious. "Why did you do it in the first place?"

Gina answered with a slight tremor. "They know my family back home. They might hurt them. And they know my record back there. They could get me deported."

"So who protects your family now?" Sabrina made a loud grunt and shot Mancini an angry look. "Of course. Quite a network you have."

"You know what we can do," Sabrina reminded him. "Now, do you see that pretty lady at the bar? Long brown hair and green dress?" Mancini glanced toward the bar and nodded. "Go try to pick her up." He froze where he was. "You still don't trust me?" she hissed. "Now you're just being stupid, Sal. Make a move on her. Go!"

Reluctantly, he headed for the bar. Sabrina asked Gina if she was hungry but the young woman was too nervous to eat. Sabrina handed her twenty dollars for dinner and she relaxed. They watched Mancini take the stool next to the brunette at the bar. She was all smiles and whispered to him with all the usual seductive gestures. She scribbled on a piece of paper. Before he left her, they shook hands. Some of the other men at the bar congratulated him; others wondered what he had that they didn't. He returned to the table.

Mancini scanned the faces in his little entourage. "She's one of the girlfriends of Richard Williams."

"The DA!" said Barrett with a low whistle.

"Yeah. She gave me a recording. Apparently, the DA won't be any trouble." He stared at Sabrina with a mixture of qualm and awe. "You and your network are impressive."

"You're welcome, Detective." Sabrina wrapped up the agenda. "Now you two guys share telephone numbers and we're done with formalities. I need a drink." Gina, still nervous, chose to leave. They advised her to take care. Mancini promised to contact her in the morning and advised to stay home with the door locked. She immediately used the twenty dollars to hail a cab and rush home.

****

My head was spinning. The meaning of the last three years of my life was in jeopardy. I had to deal with the unfinished business. "All the talk about how we shared a deep loneliness, it was a lie."

Curtly, she replied, "It was not." She kept walking quickly and I stayed with her pace. "You knew I was his neighbor. That's why you chose me."

With a deep sigh of annoyance, she said, "There is often more than one truth." She kept rushing away.

"Stop now!" I demanded. "I need to know…"

She turned around, approached me with determination, and kissed me with a passion that could set a wet log on fire. I almost succumbed but pushed her away. "I know you're good at that. I know you can turn me on. It's your profession. I organized my life around you. I struggled with own conscience. I trusted you, dammit!"

"And I am in love with you," she yelled back at me. She took my face in her hands. "Yes, we picked you because of your proximity to Mancini. I admit that. So you were a pawn, but not only a pawn. I also saw the truth of your loneliness. I really did feel the pain in your eyes. Maybe you'll never believe me but you're one of the best men I ever met. You're gentle and caring but also a wonderful lover. I trust you. I admire the way you balanced everything. And you took risks. You helped to save hundreds of girls. Maybe thousands! Can't we swallow our pride for that?"

"OK. I'll be Mancini's messenger boy. But just tell me the truth. Do you…"

"Yes, you damned fool! I love you!" We held hands and slipped into a storefront that concealed us from the streetlights. I would continue to juggle my life. She would continue to pursue her profession, now as a Confidential Informant with the DA's blessing. The sub-programs of our crazy algorithm were coming together. Would the program crash around us? I no longer cared.

As we strolled along a popular avenue, Sabrina added a coda. "You speak about how every city is really three cities."

"Hmm."

"For me, the three cities are not just a metaphor." I listened carefully. "There's the Origination City, the source, the supply. Then you have step two, the Transit City, with boats and planes and carts. You can be held in transit for a long time, in cages or locked rooms. Finally, we get here, The Destination City, with the target customers. At those three points, the organizations are vulnerable. We track those points."

"You speak about it so casually," I noticed.

She stopped walking and turned to me. "That's because of you," she explained. "I trust you. I love you. I'm getting past the pain."

Her dark eyes glistened in the evening lights. Her soft dark tresses flowed with a new freedom. Her mystery was unfolding for me.

1

A New Family?

"I don't know why I agreed to this." Adrienne fluffed her hair while she studied her appearance in the bathroom mirror. "You're not a social worker or a foster parent!" The very notion of additional responsibilities annoyed her.

Barrett leaned against the bathroom doorframe with his arms crossed. "Look, I explained the whole thing to you. The girl is very special, and she's been through a lot: wars and refugee camps and abuse. She's a smart kid, mature for her age. She had to be, just to survive. She's really precocious."

Adrienne turned away from the mirror and flipped off the bathroom light. "So why not get her into an agency? I don't want to be a nurse again!"

Barrett laughed. "Hah! With all her experience, she'd probably nurse you! Besides, agencies are underfunded and understaffed. The girl has amazing potential. She deserves a decent education." He backed away so Adrienne could move into the dining room and take a seat at the table. Candice was seated at the table with her cell phone. They could hear Glenn in the yard with Ernie.

"This must be some important client," she noted as she leaned back with her elbow on the arm of the chair and her fingers rubbing her chin. "I hope you're getting a stipend for this."

Barrett explained it one more time. "Of course. The insurance business covers a lot of situations. We'll get sufficient compensation for sure."

The doorbell rang and Barrett went to respond. Adrienne called out for Glenn to join the meeting. Barrett was expecting Gizem to be accompanied by someone representing a childcare agency. He never expected to find Sabrina standing at the entrance with her ward. Barrett was frozen in place, at a loss for words, so Sabrina filled the vacuum.

"Hello. I'm Judy Harrison from Child Protective Services." Sabrina flashed her official ID card and gave Barrett time to recover his voice.

"Of course," he said nervously. "Please come in."

Sabrina was dressed in a fashionable jade pantsuit. Her hair was tied back in a bun. Her briefcase was strapped across her shoulder. The dark-rimmed eyeglasses were pushing the stereotype to the limit. Gizem wore a modest vanilla white blouse with puffy sleeves. Her pleaded midi skirt was the color of burgundy. Her hair was entwined into two dark pigtails.

Glenn came running inside with Ernie panting behind him. "Hey, Mom! Ernie learned how to catch when I hit the ball and..." He went silent when he noticed the two females in the alcove. "Oh. You're the new girl?"

Sabrina smiled at the boy. Gizem spoke with feigned reticence. "Hello," she replied in stifled tones and lowered eyes. "My name is Gizem." The perfect little actress fidgeted with her pigtails. Barrett glared at Sabrina, who continued to smile patiently.

"Gizem?" asked Glenn. "Hmm. That's a new one." He went silent.

Adrienne broke the awkward tension. "Please have a seat," she implored. "Would you like some coffee?" Both Sabrina and Gizem answered, "Yes." Gizem bit her lip. Sabrina laughed pleasantly.

Glenn looked pained. "They let you drink coffee?" he asked Gizem, who replied with an awkward nod. Glenn frowned at his Mom.

When Adrienne went to the coffee machine, Barrett asked to see "Ms. Judy Harrison's" ID card once more. "Of course", she replied. Barrett was impressed by the authenticity of the forgery that even had the official stamp. "I don't think you appreciate the extent of our organization," she added for his ears only.

"I do now," he replied. "Please sit down."

While the coffee was brewing, Adrienne brought pound cake to the table, along with milk and sugar. Candice volunteered to retrieve some cups and dishes. Glenn eagerly grabbed a slice of the cake and Gizem cautiously followed his lead. "Is it OK, Judy?" she asked with drama.

"Of course, my dear," replied Sabrina as she shot a naughty smile to Barrett, who made sure to place himself at a safe distance from her.

Sabrina opened her briefcase and removed a "case record". Adrienne poured the coffee.

Candice was curious about the shy girl with obsidian eyes. "Where are you from, Gizem? What country?"

Her reply was well rehearsed. "I was born near Tbilisi in the Caucasus region." The bewildered expressions around the table induced her to elaborate. "Between the Black Sea and the Caspian Sea. In Georgia."

"Georgia?" asked Glenn. "Like in the Beatles song. Georgia on my mind?"

"Actually," stated Candice, "The Beatles were mocking an old song. And it was about the state of Georgia."

Glenn frowned. "I knew that," he grumbled.

Adrienne asked Gizem about her family. Sabrina answered for her charge by handing Adrienne the case record. "As you'll see, Gizem has had a difficult journey." Barrett moved closer to Adrienne and they read the record together. The family was allegedly caught up in a terrible conflict that was a combination of civil war, a struggle for independence, a religious war, and a battle between tribes and cartels. There were reports of trauma and physical abuse. Gizem is apparently the only survivor from her family. Adrienne's resistance was melting as rapidly as her sympathy for Gizem was increasing. Gizem leaned into Sabrina and began to whimper. Sabrina stroked her head affectionately.

Candice moved toward Adrienne. "What's it say, Mom?" she asked. Glenn was riveted to his chair, not knowing how to respond to such open pain.

Adrienne offered a revised version. "Gizem was trapped in a war and lost her family. She was rescued by the UN."

"Wow!" exclaimed Glenn. "The United Nations."

Adrienne shushed him and closed the case file. She turned to Barrett. "Trafficking," she murmured. "Protected herself with a knife. She's not even nine years old yet!" She turned to Gizem. "Welcome to our home, child." She looked at "Ms. Harrison" and asked, "Will you be making regular visits?"

"Of course," replied Sabrina. "The agency wants to assure a smooth transition." She looked toward Barrett who was avoiding eye contact.

"You have a business card?" asked Adrienne. "So I can call you if I have to?" Barrett felt a cold sweat across his chest.

"Certainly," answered Sabrina. She handed one to both Adrienne and Barrett. Barrett realized the card displayed a different number. Apparently Sabrina had the situation covered.

"Hey, Mom," Candice jumped in. "Can I show Gizem our rooms?"

"Yeah," answered Adrienne. "That's a good idea."

"Cool." Candice stood up, went to Gizem, and took her hand. "C'mon. Don't be shy." They climbed the stairway. As they ascended, Gizem said, "Perhaps you could show me the bathroom first?" Candice giggled and agreed.

Barrett and Adrienne watched the kids climb the stairway. Glenn decided to go to his world globe to find Tbilisi, the Black Sea and the Caspian Sea. "Interesting girl," noted Adrienne. "This was an exciting day. First Amanda's job offer and now this."

Barrett hadn't heard the news. "What about Amanda?"

"She called this morning with some news. She may get a job as a model!"

"Oh?"

"Yeah. It was so sudden. They liked her right away! They're taking her to a shoot in a few days."

"What?"

"They even offered to drive her to the site in a private limo! Can you imagine?"

"Yeah," replied Barrett with anxiety. "Yeah, I can. What's the name of the agency? Do you have their information?"

****

Glenn ran into the girls' room with his globe. "Wow! Look at this." He placed the globe on their dresser and pointed. "See? Here's The Black Sea. And this is The Caspian Sea. But I can't find Ta-bul-sky."

Gizem giggled. "Tbilisi." She directed his attention. "Right there."

Candice leaned in to scrutinize the sphere. "I don't know anything about that place. Will you teach me?" Gizem nodded.

Glenn's focus was captured by a raggedy object on the bureau. "What's that thing?" he asked with a grimace.

Gizem became solemn and moved to the bureau. She picked up the object and stroked it tenderly. "It's a doll," she replied. "Well, it was a doll for me. It helps me to remember…things."

Glenn thought for a second and asked, "What's 'trafficking'? Is it bad?"

18

The False Tip

As usual, Nobody's was comfortably barren except for several familiar locals and a few nervous newbies. The bartender didn't have to ask about the regulars' orders and poured them "the usual". Coo sat with Tabby at their discreet corner booth. Coo was crossing her legs like a true professional but Tabby was approached first. Coo sneered playfully as her colleague exchanged insults with the guy. It served as some kind of initiation and he passed the test. She knew what he wanted; but Tabby needed a few drinks before further commitments. He readily obliged her thirst.

Coo didn't much care for beer, especially the gunk sold at Nobody's. She nursed a Chardonnay slowly while Tabby and the customer increased their fondling between gulps of suds. She was glad when Sabrina arrived and sat next to her. With a nod, the bartender poured out her familiar cocktail.

Renee delivered the drink with her usual flair. "Gin and tonic for my favorite girl."

Sabrina thanked her with an alluring expression. She was preferring female companions at the moment. "You're not busy. Sit with me."

"With us," Coo corrected her. "But maybe not for long," she added as a good-looking Latino meandered to their booth. There was something underhanded about him; but, then again, Coo was not the refined type either. He spoke in a husky voice with macho arrogance. "Your friend might earn her money right here on the table," he snorted as he watched Tabby and her patron. When they turned to him, he challenged the other man with a savage stare. The alpha male won the contest. The couple decided to relocate. As they slogged away, Latino grunted, "Punk." His face was frozen, as if a force field insulated him from the world. Renee, always attuned to trouble, shifted her attention to the booth. With his hand on Coo's leg, Alpha looked at Sabrina. "Join us," he ordered with a somber voice that proclaimed someone used to being obeyed.

"No thank you," she replied with forced civility. "I'm spending time with my girlfriend tonight." She winked at Renee.

The waitress glided over to their booth. "That's right, Carlos. It's Ladies' Night." She brushed Sabrina's cheek.

"Dykes," he groused. "My name ain't Carlos. It's Angel."

"Oh yeah," replied Renee, "That fits." The air grew tense.

Coo tried to distract him. "C'mon, Angel. Let's take a walk."

But Angel pushed her away. "Bitches. Proud whores. Dime a dozen!" He slumped back in his seat. "You got a lot of competition comin'. Real soon. Younger, prettier. Won't be so proud then."

Sabrina looked at him with razor eyes. "What are you saying?"

"You're dark, like midnight. I'll call you that." She could smell whiskey on his breath. "Yeah, Midnight. Three truckloads." He slurred his words but she caught them. "From different towns. They all meet tomorrow. At the trading house."

Renee pulled back silently. Sabrina remained attentive. Coo had a searching expression. "Trading house? What the…" Sabrina quieted her with a raised hand and a furtive look.

"Bullshit," mumbled Sabrina. "You talkin' trash."

"Yeah, right," the Latino countered. "Three o'clock tomorrow. The old school that was abandoned. On Cornwall." He was fading fast into an alcohol stupor. "Lotta Asian competition soon for you bitches…" But then, in a determined effort, he roused himself and disengaged from Coo. "Hell with it. Later for you. Too much trouble. Don't need your ass. I got plenty..." He staggered out of the bar.

Renee watched him leave with relief. "Good buy to bad trash," she proclaimed.

Coo was ambivalent. "He was nasty, but he was wasted. I coulda made easy money on that one."

"No, baby," cautioned Sabrina. "That was a bad honcho."

Renee was fixed in thought. "What'd he say about Asians?"

"He was rambling," answered Sabrina. "Drunk and wasted, like Coo says. Telling lies to impress us ladies, even if we are 'bitches and ho's'."

"Think he'll come back?" wondered Coo. "Sometimes they feel offended, and return, maybe with a gun."

"I don't think so," replied Renee. "Never seen him here before. What about you?" She turned to the bartender. He answered with, "No way."

"Yeah," said Sabrina with stealth. "A stranger. Won't even remember this bar. It's not easy to find this place even when you're sober." She gazed at Renee. "You have to go home to the kids?" Wistfully, the waitress nodded. "C'est la vie." It was a quiet night from then on. Sabrina and Coo shared a cab.

****

Barrett was sitting at the bar and watching the large screen TV with the rest of the crowd. Two other men were studying the game like forensic analysts. He wondered how the world might change if they paid as much attention to political events. Mancini walked in and traipsed over to him. "What's the score?" he asked.

"How the hell do I know?" Barrett vented. "I'm just watching the action. Anyway, I'm thinking of something else."

"I bet you are," Mancini retorted. "Let's get a table." They moved to the rear. The noise in the place served as a sound wall. Nothing they said would be overheard. "So why the late call?"

"Some loudmouth at Nobody's got drunk and chatty. Sabrina thinks it's important. It's going down at three o'clock."

"This happened tonight? And something's happening tomorrow? Not enough time to check sources." Mancini grew pensive. "I'll bring a few cops and a cameraman."

"Yeah. The old schoolhouse on Cornwall? You know it?"

Mancini grunted. "Hmm. Bunch of homeless guys and druggies." He saw the waitress approaching. "We better order drinks."

Barrett made his order and glanced at the TV. "So who's winning?"

Mancini was curt. "I hope we are."

****

Right on time, the three trucks converged in the parking lot of the old schoolhouse. When the doors were opened, several women emerged from each truck. Mancini whispered to the cameraman, "You getting' this?" He nodded. Mancini made a quick count and estimated the size of the operation. "OK. Let's move in. Carefully."

Five cops and Mancini flanked the scene. "Hold it right there! Police. Freeze!" The drivers raised their hands and laughed. The women acted confused and frightened. "Open up the trucks? How many more in there?"

The lead driver acted dumbfounded. "What you lookin' for?" The cops entered the vehicles with searchlights and their guns ready. They came out with the look of chagrin.

"Blankets and coats," said the sergeant. "Just clothes."

Mancini was not convinced. "Could be covering drugs. Look it all over."

After a thorough search, police and suspects relaxed. The leader of the operation offered an explanation. "We're a private group that brings stuff to the homeless populations. We do these drops. Mind if I smoke?"

"Go ahead," replied Mancini. "Sorry about the confusion. But you gotta admit, it looked suspicious."

"No harm done," replied the driver. "It made the run a lot more exciting."

144

The passengers in the police van were silent as they returned to headquarters. Mancini was unsettled about the incident. "It doesn't add up," he murmured to the sergeant.

"No. Not at all. Why is some macho drunk braggin' about a clothing drop? What's the point?"

"A large trafficking organization gets nailed at the pier. A few weeks later, a guy pulls this joke. My sources didn't have time to check it out. So we get suckered."

"Someone trying to bring us down? Make us look bad?"

"Maybe." Mancini felt an icy chill. "It was a test! Since the pier, they're trying to find the leak! Shit!" He made a quick phone call and stepped on the accelerator. "My assets are in trouble," he muttered through clenched teeth.

19

Turnabout

Sabrina walked into Nobody's Bar, winked at the bartender, and gave Renee a quick wave. The place was busier than usual. Probably some legal holiday, she figured, as she sought some restrained solitude among the chatter. Tabby was occupied at the bar with a tourist from the Mid-West and their usual booth was filled with a couple of writers who were clicking away on their laptops between swigs of beer.

Someone tapped her on her shoulder and spoke in a controlled rough voice. "Have a seat, Squirrel. It's been a long time." The tap changed into a tight grip.

Sabrina felt a tingling paresthesia jab at her fingers and toes. Her tongue went dry and her knees began to quiver. Although the bar was warm, she felt like she was packed in ice. She couldn't control her shivering.

"Don't bother with the frightened girl routine, Squirrel. Sit." With forced tranquility, she took a seat beside two bulky men. But it was the voice behind her that tossed her into a well of resurgent trauma.

Squirrel. No one had called her by that name since…while she lay there, bound, exposed, helpless – her tormentor was fascinated by her eyes. "You ever stare at squirrel?" he asked. "They have your eyes, slit and totally dark. It's like looking into the black stone of Mecca. Astarte's rock." He spoke to her like they were friends. He was getting poetic about her appearance. She was naked and trembling as he glided a gun across her thighs. "A wild pagan," he seethed like an angry snake. He ran his fingers across her cheek. "Black opal," he whispered like a lover. "Reflecting it all back at me." The gun roamed across her belly and climbed to circle her breasts. "So exotic! So enticing! You're worth a fortune, my squirrel." With that remark, Sabrina's affect shifted. She was valuable; she had leverage. He wouldn't damage the merchandise.

The past and the present merged into primal rage. But Sabrina had to be cool. She was determined to reveal nothing. She sat down and looked into the face of a buried nightmare that had returned to torment her once again. He was her custodian in the trading house. He bargained with other gangs and exchanged many women. But she was his prize. He wouldn't deal her. It would take a sheik or a wealthy oilman to purchase her.

"I always wondered how you got away," he snarled. "You and that brat. You're a sly squirrel. Well, it's time to come home." She froze and the two men at her sides pressed into her. "You don't want to make a scene, Squirrel. By the time any one knows you were stabbed, it would be too late." She complied and left the bar with her escorts. Renee and the bartender noticed her leaving quietly with three men.

In the unassuming Toyota, no suspicion was aroused. It was a very quiet drive. They crossed the river and arrived at an old factory complex. Beyond the brick façade and fire escapes was a large chamber that was decorated only by exposed pipes and sharp fluorescents. Several metal doors opened to adjourning corridors.

They sat Sabrina on a heavy metal chair and bound her arms. "Just like old times, eh?" He snarled with a grotesque smirk. Then he got down to business. "I don't want to hurt you. But I will. When that cargo at the pier was busted, we lost a lot of money. Some very important people are very angry." He brushed his hand through her thin dark hair. "Just give me some names I can work with. People need a refund." He leaned in and kissed her. "Beautiful black opal. You could have been my woman."

Sabrina retorted with spit flying from her mouth. "You branded me! You laughed when they shaved me! You lock women up like wild beasts! And now you adore me? Now you're my soul-mate?"

With gun in hand, he raised her skirt. "Yes. My brand." He studied the revision. "Nicely concealed, Squirrel. Yeah, you have the spirit of a snake; the way you just slithered away from me." Her eyes were fixed upon him like a poised cobra. "You'd like to scratch my eyes out, wouldn't you?" Playtime was over. He raised the gun to her face. "Names, Squirrel. Now!"

She closed her eyes and began to pant. "I need some water, please. I think I'm gonna faint."

"Sure," he replied. "Anything for my girl." He turned to a nearby sink.

He was about three feet away from her as he turned on the faucet.

The microchip recorder, embedded deep within her arm, had done its job. The SWAT team flooded the chamber. Sabrina's eyes were burning when the gas canisters exploded. Automatic weapon fire echoed and ricocheted across the loggia. Some of the traffickers dropped their weapons; others fell bleeding. The battle continued through the corridors where gunfire blended with the sound of women screaming.

He was slumped on the ground, wounded, and he glared at Sabrina with a hatred that would cross several lifetimes. Crawling toward her, he raised his gun and pointed it. Still bound to the immobile interrogation chair, Sabrina took a deep breath and found a place inside, a place of peace and love, a place she shared with Barrett, a calm sanctuary removed from pain.

The sharpshooter interceded, wearing a gas mask, and pointing his rifle at him. "Halt!" But he was too filled with animus to stop. The rifle rapped its deadly staccato. The officer released Sabrina and she began to scream. Other women, liberated from their cells, came rushing through the metal doors. She couldn't contain her shrieks. Running to her prone tormentor, she grabbed the gun near his body.

Still wailing, she pulled the trigger again and again. The sharpshooters surrounded her but let her catharsis play out. When the bullets were spent, she dropped the gun. Lightheaded, she looked around the hall at all the women and girls. The sharpshooter caught her as she swooned.

****

Tabby had finished her work with the Mid-Western tourist. Customers were getting comfortably drunk as they watched the large-screen TVs around the bar. Most of them were focused on the latest sports drama. Renee and the bartender happened to zone into the news channel near the back bar. A major trafficking bust had taken place in south Jersey at an old factory site. Information was spotty but the police action was extensive. In other news, the realtor Henry Anderson agreed on a two million dollar settlement regarding illegal immigrant labor. Mr. Anderson denied any guilt and shrugged it off as a technical violation.

The bartender cursed as he wiped the counter. "That guy probably took two million out of his wallet. Meanwhile, some poor bastards hide in boats just to earn two dollars a day."

Renee nodded her agreement. "The whole damn economy's screwed up."

The bartender laughed sardonically. "Not for Henry Anderson."

In more regional news, D.A. Richard Williams completely denied rumors of a sexual liaison with an under-age female. Allegedly, the girl had evidence.

20

Making A Scene

I tried to push the images out of my head. But all the tales kept racing across my mind. Adrienne grumbled as I kept disrupting her sleep. So I slipped into Amanda's room for the night. I looked around at all the tokens of her childhood. Her favorite doll, the one she just had to have for Christmas when she was nine years old, was now tossed in the far corner, next to the unicorn that she clung to at ten. On her shelf were the trophies from lacrosse, softball, and volleyball. On her desk were scrapbooks with drawings and photographs. I glanced over her favorite books and remembered reading some of them to her. She was an alert listener and often asked questions when the chapter was done.

Gizem was only seven when…Sabrina was lured into the trap with a job offer…They provided a car…

I remember when Amanda started to mature. Adrienne and I would comment about her development and worry about the attention she'd get. She looked good in a bikini on the beach. I would wait up for her to return from dates. I did my best to be casual about them, but my anxiety was obvious.

Some of the "customers" were fond of young girls…A lot of the trafficking is domestic…The young women are naïve and vulnerable…

It was useless to try to sleep. I took a shower and a shave. I left a message at the day job; family issues, I said. I put on clothes that were casual but neat. Stopping at the gas station, I filled a thermos of coffee and bought a buttered roll.

As I cashed out, a young girl, maybe sixteen at most, eyed me with a smile. It was around three in the morning. Her mascara was running and her hairspray was excessive. We made eye contact. I wanted to tell her to go home, to get away from the pimp who was compelling her performance. Maybe she was waiting for a stranger she contacted on an "adult" web site. Hell, I was tempted to scold her, like an Old Testament Prophet! The cashier got impatient with me. "Excuse me, sir," he said in a surly tone. "Your change." Then he added with a sneer, "Unless you want something else?" Was the cashier her pimp? Racing to rescue my daughter, I was confronted by another standoff. What if I just walked away and the girl shows up in tomorrow's newspaper?

I turned to the girl. "Are you OK?" I asked her.

She nodded her head nervously. "Yeah. I'll be fine," she sniveled. "Thanks for asking." Was that her code for, "Help me"? I'm still a novice at this crap! If only Sabrina were here…

"All right," was all I could muster. "You take care of yourself."

With a full tank of gas, and a brain full of caffeine, I drove through the night and reached Amanda's campus by dawn. The security guard at the gate approached my car suspiciously. I eagerly showed him my ID which he perused carefully. He took my license and returned to his gatehouse to make a few calls. I was annoyed at the delay but also thankful for the cautious college policies. A sleepy student introduced herself. She was a senior and Amanda's dorm leader. The DL directed me to wait in the kitchen while she went to Amanda's room. I nibbled on some crackers on the table.

The DL returned with a black student named Charlene. She introduced herself and yawned. "You're Amanda's father?" I answered in a rush. "She went with Gilbert, her boyfriend." Charlene went to the sink for a drink of water.

"Where?" I asked desperately. "Where did they go?"

"A job interview," replied the girl who sensed my anxiety. "Why? What's wrong?"

"Nothing, I hope," I replied. "Just tell me where they went." My tone grew insistent.

"Hey, chill out for a minute, OK?" Charlene put up her hands. "I think Irene told her about the job. She'll know."

"OK, fine. Where's Irene?"

Charlene got nervous and the DL intervened. "Irene is probably with her boyfriend." She turned to Charlene, who shrugged.

I got flustered. "Look! I need to find her. It could be urgent. She's not answering her phone! Why wouldn't she answer her phone?"

The senior tried to reassure me. "Listen, Mr. Sherman. Gil is a good guy. If she went with him, he's reliable. I'll check the student roster for his phone number." I thanked her.

Cynthia and a rather taciturn girl showed up next. "What's going on? You woke us up, man! It's too early for breakfast." She rubbed her eyes.

On impulse, I asked, "Do you have Gil's number?"

To the surprise of every one, she said, "Yes. Why? Something happen?"

I was trying to contain my panic. "Please, Cynthia, just let me have Gil's number."

It turned out that the DL and Cynthia retrieved his number simultaneously. Cynthia made the call and explained the situation to him. "Mr. Sherman? Amanda's Dad?" he asked with a mixture of confusion and fear. "Hello, how are you?" He described where he was and told me that Amanda was picked up early for a sunrise photo shoot at a nearby nature preserve.

****

She was standing on a mountain ledge with her arms extended and legs apart. A wind machine was blowing her hair. Below her was the dense valley. The crew was holding reflectors and light meters. The photographer was taking numerous pictures from several angles.

"That's great, girl!" he exclaimed. "Now put your hands in your hair, ya know? Yeah, that's it. You are a natural!"

I ran to the scene and the crew was startled by my frazzled appearance. Amanda came out of her pose and stared at me in disbelief. "Dad? What are you doing here?"

How could I explain the terror? How could I make her understand my reaction? When do you decide if a job is a normal enterprise or a planned abduction? I was embarrassed and exhausted. I stammered out some rationale. "I called you. You didn't answer."

Amanda came off the ledge and examined my demeanor. "You called me? When?"

"I dunno. Maybe two AM," I answered sheepishly. Amanda and the entire crew were now poring over my appearance.

"Why would you call me at two in the morning?" She looked worried.

"Of course I would," I replied. "The job offer. The private car. All the secrecy."

"Dad, what's wrong?" She was scrutinizing a madman.

I felt weak and got dizzy. "I need to sit down," I murmured. One of the crewmembers led me to a chair. "When I have the chance to explain, you'll understand."

Amanda called Gil to inform him I'd be staying with them for the morning.

When is it paranoia and when is it real? The modern slavery is all around us but we're blinded by our own prejudices. When the scales fall from our eyes, the nightmares become real. Somehow, you have to find a path through the whirlpool.

Amanda explained how the early shoot was for the sunrise effect. They were planning to put the image on a popular yoga magazine. "You know it, Dad," she elaborated. "The one Mom subscribes to. I was hoping to surprise her."

The circle keeps spinning. "OK. I won't tell her about it," I replied. I also wanted to see the expression on Adrienne's face when the magazine arrived in the mail.

Back at the dorm, I told her about Gizem's history. I explained that, once I learned about the poor girl's traumatic experiences, I began doing my own research. The more I read, the more horrifying it got. "So I hope you understand. The similarities in the pattern just got to me. I over-reacted this time. I'm so sorry."

Amanda moved in and embraced me. "I get it, Dad. You love me, you care about me." We held each other with a shared love that required no words. When we disengaged, she said, "I'm appreciating Gil even more now. On some intuitive level, he felt the need to protect me too."

I chortled. "Tell Gil he has my blessings."

****

Driving home from the college, I reviewed what Amanda tried to teach me about Quantum mechanics. Matter isn't really material at all; instead all matter is actually waves. But, when a particle passes through the Higgs Field, it gains mass. There are particles called bosons that are actually forces. But particles of matter are called fermions. There are also virtual particles that pop in and out of existence from a surrounding field. There may actually be a parallel universe in which we live a different reality. You also have "entanglement"; particles can affect each other despite the distance between them. Somehow these baffling concepts helped to clarify my current reality.

Epilogue

B arrett sat in his armchair and watched Adrienne playing chess with Gizem. He was surprised and somewhat disconcerted by the ease with which the strange young girl had assimilated into his family and won their hearts. Amanda was intrigued when she visited for the holidays and displayed no resistance to sharing her room. Glenn would often laugh with her and was thankful for the extra help with math. But, most of all, Adrienne's attachment to their new resident was singular. She had brightened since the girl entered her life.

When they went to the local school to register Gizem, the procedure went smoothly. Sabrina's organization had wonderful forgers: the girl's folder contained her birth certificate, passport, and visa. In addition, some very official-looking documents declared her special refugee status; and designated Adrienne and Barrett as her legal guardians. According to Sabrina, the legitimate NGO on some documents actually did help. Sabrina put together a reasonably accurate psychosocial history. Few human beings could read it without shedding a tear and offering enthusiastic support. She was nine years old but, based on her admission ratings, was skipped to the fifth grade.

The girl's ability to handle peers was astounding. When other children approached her with preconceived notions, she managed to clarify things in a very direct but pleasant manner. Despite a few early playground incidents, Gizem was accepted. Several girls her age were perturbed by Gizem's gender-neutral choice of close friends. While most of her peers stayed in girl groups, Gizem compiled a faction of boys and girls. Some Guidance Counselors found that to be "overly precocious", but most of the teachers liked the model of diversity and inclusion.

The chess game was close for a while; but once Gizem gained the center, it was a foregone conclusion. After a shrewd maneuver to checkmate, they shook hands and reviewed a few moves. Grabbing a piece of fruit from the kitchen, Gizem went to her room to finish her homework. She child still preferred reading books to watching TV. Adrienne approached Barrett and sat next to him. She was relaxed and wore a grin. Barrett witnessed the significant decrease in tension.

He smiled. "You really like that girl, don't you?" He wrapped his arms around her and Adrienne did not resist.

Adrienne nodded. "She's a wonderful child. I think how much she had to endure. She's a tough survivor, but she's so sweet." Her next remark made a deep impression on Barrett. "Thank you for bringing her into our home."

Barrett's parallel lives were hopscotching over each other. It was becoming a painful balancing act for him. "Her social worker should get most of the credit. Gizem was one of the lucky ones. She had a family legacy."

Adrienne studied Barrett. "That's where your insurance agency got involved."

"Yeah." Barrett had repeated the tale many times. "Once I was introduced to that girl, I knew what we had to do."

Adrienne glided closer to him. "You made a decision from the heart," she purred. "I'm glad you did. It means a lot to me." Barrett turned to observe his wife, who had the expression of a penitent. "I've been through a lot of changes. Physically, my body just doesn't …" She paused and pursed her lips. Barrett placed his hand on her shoulder to offer reassurance. Adrienne continued. "Amanda, all full of life, goes off to college. It's like I feel unhinged. Candi does her thing and Glenn is in his own world…"

Barrett helped her to finish the thought. "So Gizem is filling a gap, eh?"

Adrienne grew pensive. "When I had the abortion, it was the right choice. Now I know why. I was holding a place for Gizem."

Barrett reacted with a gasp. Adrienne struggled to explicate. "Don't misunderstand. I know I can't get too dependent on her. But for now…"

"A transitional object," Barrett added. "A significant time in all our lives. We're all in a transition. Gizem needs us for the same reason."

"So every one benefits." Adrienne liked that conclusion. "Perhaps we should invite Ms. Harrison to dinner some time."

Barrett was momentarily confused. "Excuse me? Who?"

"Judy Harrison," replied Adrienne. "Her social worker. We should stay on good terms with her. If we think about adoption…"

Barrett's thoughts went into pretzel twists. Would that be a good thing, he pondered, or a disaster? Would it provide him with more flexibility or open the door to chaos? "I'm not sure," he stated. "She probably has to maintain a professional boundary. It might violate her ethics."

"Nonsense!" exclaimed Adrienne. "When a social worker is dealing with the benefit of a child, she wants to be involved with the placement family." Then she softened. "We could ask her."

'I guess so," replied Barrett, caught in a checkmate. "What harm could it do?"

Credits and References

This novel is based on numerous actual sources. I want to acknowledge at least some of them.

Thank you to Peggy Belles, a retired New York police officer, who is now a dietician and a yoga instructor, for her help in describing police procedures and policies.

A shout out to New York Times journalist Nicholas Kristof. Since 2004, he has been reporting on sex trafficking, especially of young girls. His articles are available online.

Cavalieri, Shelley, "Between Victim and Agent: A Third-Way Feminist Account of Trafficking for Sex Work", Indiana Law Journal, Maurer School of Law, 86:4, Fall 2011. wattn@indiana.edu

DeStefano, Anthony M., "The War on Human Trafficking – US Policy Assessed", Rutgers University Press, 2007.

Edited by Obi N.I. Ebbe & Dilip K. Das: "Global Trafficking in Women and Children", CRC Press, Taylor & Francis Group, Boca Raton, London, New York. 2008 (17 powerful research articles by several authors).

I salute NY Senator Kirsten Gillibrand, who introduced in Congress:

The Trafficking Survivors Relief Act of 2016.

Goldberg, Eleanor, "Here's How Easy it is For Human Traffickers to Transport Victims into the US", The Huffington Press, 10/23/2014.

Edited by Maggie Lee, "Human Trafficking", Willan Publishing, NY, 2007 and Routledge, London, 2011.

Little, Dr. Stacey, "Transportation's Critical Role in Fighting Human Trafficking", American Public University. Also in a brochure by InPublicSafety.com (published by American Military University).

Lloyd, Rachel, former sex worker and founder of Girls Educational and Mentoring Services (GEMS) in 1998. She was interviewd by FORBES Magazine journalist Meghan Casserly on January 24th, 2012.

Trafficking Map "Coming to America" distributed by the U.S. State Department, The Protection Project. Graphic by Dave Eames and Mark Morris, The Kansas City Star, 2009.

Newsweek Magazine: "Smuggled for Sex", series 1999-2001

Powell, Andrea, "Why Do We Lock Up Survivors of Sex Trafficking?" 9/28/2016. Ms. Powell is the founder and executive director of FAIR Girls.

Tan, Carol, "Does Legalized Prostitution Increase Human Trafficking?", Harvard Kennedy School, Shorenstein Center on Media, Politics, and Public Policy.

Info borrowed from: Cho, Seo-Young; Dreher, Axel; Neumayer, Eric; "Does Legalized Prostitution Increase Human Trafficking?" World Development, 2013, 41:67-82.

Protocols declared by The United Nations (UN) and the International Labor Organization (ILO).

The United Nations Global Initiative to Fight Human Trafficking (UN.GIFT), 2007, with cooperation of ILO, UNICEF, and International Organization for Migration (IOM) (originally funded by The United Arab Emirates).

OHCHR = Office of the UN High Commission for Human Rights.

OSCE = Organization for Security and Cooperation in Europe.

UNODC = UN Office on Drugs and Crime. UNODC Report: "Global Report on Trafficking in Persons"; 12/21/2016. Executive Director, Yuri Fedotov.

The front cover image for this novel was edited. The original stock photo is from: Blend Images/John Lund/Stephanie Roeser. #BLD092127. Revisions were made by RUSH Graphics in Hawthorne, New Jersey.

About the Author

Steven R Green is a retired clinical social worker who lives in New York. He specialized for many years in treatment in women's issues, eating disorders, and trauma. He has a web page with a blog at www.stevenrbtgreen.com.

Other Novels By Steven R Green:

Beyond The Lock (originally published as "Interlock")

(Telepathy, Mental Health Treatment, CompuThink, and Human Evolution)

Menage3 (A loving threesome who conquer obstacles)

Menage3B – Baby Makes Four (sequel to Menage3)

The eBook versions are available on Amazon, Barnes&Noble, Kobo, and Smashwords.